BACK SO SOON?
AND OTHER STORIES

Richard Passmore

RICHARD PASSMORE

Back so Soon?
and other stories

Thomas Harmsworth Publishing
Stoke Abbott

By the same author:
Blenheim Boy
Moving Tent
Thursday is Missing

British Library Cataloguing in Publication Data
Passmore, Richard, *1920–*
    Back so soon? and other stories.
    I. Title
    823'.914 [F]

    ISBN 0-948807-09-1

Printed in Great Britain by:
Bookcraft Bath Ltd.

Contents

Contents

1

Back so soon?

That time They let me die peaceably in my bed: I simply went
to sleep one night and woke up dead. The easiest way to go, of
course. Once I had left the body behind I lingered for a last look
around – there had been some good moments, as always – and
then sped on my way to report-in with Azrael's department. As
I crossed the Threshold my cumulative memory was again
reactivated; it was then that I realised that this past life was
the first time I had been English. Last time, I now knew, I had
been a Boer woman and had died of typhus in an English
concentration-camp, out on the veldt, near Bloemfontein. Then
we had thought of the English as devils incarnate and had hated
them totally, and with reason enough. But now that I had
experienced what it was like to be English, and a man, I could
understand them better. Now I knew of the peculiar inhibitions
and superstitions which motivated them – these made more
potent by a huge and unquestioned assumption that only
English values were truly civilised. Peculiar, very.

Before my Boer incarnation I had been some kind of Serbian
peasant (or was it Bosnian?) At any rate I had saved the life of
the Emperor Franz Joseph I by shielding him from a sniper's
bullet – at the Battle of Solferino, I think it was. He had at once
commissioned me as a full lieutenant and raised me to the
nobility as (I think I remember it correctly) Ritter von Trotta.
Not that it did me much good: within a few more weeks I had
died from a very painful sword-thrust, at some minor skirmish.

1

I rapidly reviewed mentally several more incarnations, ranged back one by one into the earliest days (*my* earliest days, anyhow). The first, I think, was as a hoplite of Tiglath Pilezer; the Third, of course: where would Assyria have been without him? So many lives: so many destinies. I could only hope that The Boss knew what he was about with me.

So I checked-in and was debriefed. What did I consider my major achievement this time? Of what did I accuse myself? What faults would I seek to eradicate when my next incarnation was due? And so on.

After all this was over I went over to the stores and reclaimed my halo, found my quarters, was given a timetable for the immediate future and went out for a spot of casting-down. While this activity was hard to rationalise – for some of us, at any rate – yet it was rumoured that The Boss was rather keen that we should all do a stint occasionally, perhaps (I suppose) by way of a loyalty-test. And whatever you were tempted to feel about it or (even more dangerously) *say* about it, you had to keep in mind the possibility that The Boss sometimes monitored the thought-waves.

Today, I found, casting-down was off. The Glassy Sea* was closed while a considerable number of golden crowns were recovered, refurbished and made ready for casting back. The beach offered a few undecided entities wondering what to do now in order to pick-up a few credits: it was widely (and perhaps erroneously) held that the number of credits you notched-up between incarnations was instrumental in deter-mining the particular form of your next operational trip. After all, who wanted to be an Eskimo or a Chinese peasant? There was, of course, perpetual discussion about what constituted the ideal posting but with my last trip in mind I now considered it would be hard to beat the life of an English bourgeois. This last time I had been sent to one of the two (supposedly) best schools, from which I went on to the (supposedly) best college

* Revelation Ch4 vv6,10

at one of the two (supposedly) best universities. Harrow and Trinity College Cambridge, of course. As a consequence I had emerged from this highly formative period with a mind from which unpleasant realities were easily and firmly excluded. Things were as things jolly well ought to be and that was, quite simply, that. The chain of reasoning was impressively simple:

i. In a well-ordered universe some unpleasantnesses ought not to be.

ii. This is a well-ordered universe (it is for the bourgeoisie, at any rate), so

iii. Unpleasantnesses simply do not exist, and further

iv. Any contrary indication not only might be ignored but *must* by all right-minded people be ignored.

Although such habits of mind were often (by such as the French) condemned as hypocritical intolerance, yet they were not so much intolerant as simply dismissive. An English gentleman wore a suit of armour impenetrable to realists – but then, who in his right mind wants to be a realist? Happiness consists in being protected by a shock-absorber of pleasing illusion.

Anyway, it was a lovely afternoon and I was soon sitting in the Transients' Lounge, boning-up on my latest dossiers; apparently I had completed seven missions and was to be prepared, in a leisurely fashion, for an eighth. I was in no hurry to go terrene again so soon: the heavenly climate is, of course, ideal. But I had to wonder: what would I be next time? Yet there was no hurry, as I have said: the customary post-operational rest-and-recuperation period would be a pleasant break.

Looking idly out of the window I observed that the Glassy Sea was now once more open for business: perhaps later I might . . . The Archivist was fussing mildly around; like all storekeepers he was never at ease until all his stock was neatly arranged in its proper order: he kept giving me significant looks, all of which I ignored. To add to his annoyance he kept bumping the tips of his wings on the ceiling: the residents' lounge had a much higher ceiling and huge picture windows so that members of the Mess could simply fly in and out as, today, most of them would choose to do.

The Boss was in a good mood; that was obvious from the apple-green atmosphere (there could, of course, be no sky), flushed delicately with the palest pink. The unending muzak was emitting soft and harmonious sounds, very muted, rather like Bruckner bumbling along on one of his better days. I was mildly bored and after all there was no haste: I had only just returned. Across the lawn I could see the nearest stack of crowns, glinting in the light from the Throne*; several celebrants were already busily occupied, causing an almost unbroken musical splashing. Time I rousted out Charlie, I thought: he had been given to boasting about how far he could cast a crown.

Charlie, however, had other things on his mind. He was sitting some miles away on the other side of the lounge; like myself, he was mulling over his archives. His last incarnation, we all knew, had been as an illustrious Englishman: King Charles the First – and everyone knew what had happened to *him*. Charlie's Guardian Angel had been so incensed at his premature return that he had announced a long series of self-criticism sessions before Charlie would be considered for another incarnation. Faced with the prospect of endless sessions with Ahitophel, Charlie was quite desperate to get away and would have jumped at any role offered to him, no matter how unpromising. That, however, depended on satisfying his GA, and that in its turn depended on his identifying all the faults of his last, abortive, mission.

I went over and pointed out that there was a vacant patch on the shore of the GS and asked him to join me for a short spell of casting-down; all work and no play, I pointed out . . . but Charlie was not to be distracted.

* Revelation Ch21 v23

4

'Retro me Satanas,' he snarled. A bit strong, I thought: after all we *were* in Heaven and I had been thoroughly shriven after my recent return.

'But we've got to get our stint done,' I pointed out. 'The Boss expects it of us.'

'First things first,' he replied. 'Ahitophel learned yesterday evening that he had been passed-over for promotion to archangel and he blames me for it. I must show willing. Just leave me, old man: go and get in a spot of solitaire – and throw in a couple for me while you're at it.'

So I handed in my archives and did a spot of casting-down but I must confess my heart was not in it, and soon I went back to the lounge. I had hardly sat down again when there was a frightful noise somewhere outside – rather like Stockhausen in one of his more-innovative moods. Flashes of sulphurous light preceded a strange archangel down the corridor and into our lounge. The microclimate which he brought with him quite occluded the Boss's own emanations. This angry Being consulted some kind of document, lifted his head and appealed to us all.

'I'm looking for Sebastian. 354/X Sebastian, that is. He's wanted urgently. Has anyone seen him?'

Heads turned this way and that; there was a vague muttering of a distinctly negative nature.

'Oh. . . ,' he exclaimed, choking-off just in time whatever he had meant to say. 'He's needed at once for incarnating. He's overdue already – the medical team down there have started induction and there isn't a spirit ready and prepared.'

For a few seconds he stood there, fuming. We all quailed and wished him away: archangels, and especially angry archangels, were never comfortable people to have near you even if your conscience was clear. You can, of course, hardly sin in Heaven but there were minor peccadillos . . .

The Archangel made a sudden decision. He turned to the nearest chair – mine – quite overpowering me with his presence.

5

'Hey, you,' he snapped. 'Take this,' he held out the paper in his hand. 'Get yourself genned-up. You're going down right away. There isn't time for a full briefing. Read it on your way to the Despatch Department. Right, *move*.'

The last word came out like the crack of a whip and at once I found myself half-way to the door, moving at a brisk trot. What this time? Usually it took a whole day of eternity to be prepared for one's next trip – say, some seventy or so earth years; this time I would have had considerably less than that. In fact, I had barely time to skim over the salient points before urgent hands grabbed me and I was loaded into a despatch module.

It was once again to be a comfortable English family, I learned. Perhaps I would be selected to specialise in English parts? To that I had no objection; yet if only I could be French again. . . ah, the food. Still, it would be better than that dreadful incarnation as an Indian peasant: the dirt, the flies and the diseases. And the stinks. I shuddered. Professional class. Two children on the edge of their teens: I was to be an afterthought, technically known as a gap-baby. C of E: good; no irksome religious observances. Down there one never knew when one was to lose one's foreskin and abstain from pork and shellfish; or to be allowed four wives but no alcohol. . . and Ramadan! Ugh. There seemed to be utter confusion whether The Boss liked to be worshipped with or without a hat; with or without shoes on one's feet; on Saturday or on Sunday; in reverent silence, with brass bands, with candles, bells and holy smells – or to wailing noises from high towers. No doubt of it: terrenes were very mixed-up. And soon I was to be part of it all over again. At least Anglicanism was the easiest to endure. Turn up twice a year for the Rite, throw in a sub for the cubs or the Brownies or the church roof or the organ fund, have one's children splashed with water and that was all. Quite undemanding, really.

Then the capsule burst and at the precise second I suddenly realised that in the haste and confusion of my unplanned departure from Heaven They had forgotten to switch off my

6

cumulative memory. Someone had omitted to go through the landing-drill. So there I was, alive and yet totally conscious, imprisoned in a body which was, as yet, incapable of carrying-out my most elementary wishes.

It really was an ignominious situation. I was hanging upside-down; someone was holding me, none too gently, by the ankles; a large hand smacked me – I preferred not to think where. All I could manage by way of protest was a feeble, puling wail. Once I had thus signified my safe arrival I was laid on something soft, cleaned and inspected. It was totally infuriating. There I was, on my eighth incarnation: I, who had been a warrior and a nobleman and the wife of a Dutch guerrilla and an associate of a very learned society – there I was locked into a helpless body which was totally beyond my control. Even my eyes would not obey me: my surroundings swam in great, amorphous splodges of colour. This had happened on each previous incarnation, of course, but then my consciousness was no more developed than my muscular control, and over the subsequent weeks and months and years I was able to develop both at the same rate. This time my soul-case and my consciousness were wildly out of phase. At least I could sleep – and did.

For the next endless section of time I had to submit to being handled, fed 'on excrementitious obscenities'*, intimately cleaned; it was all unspeakably horrible.

I remember the shock when, for the first time, I managed to control my eyes for the few seconds enough to focus on my new mother: I was certain I recognised her. . . but who was she? Yet not long afterwards came the day when I heard her cooing, 'Here comes your Daddy.'

With a great effort I managed to control my head and my eyes; I turned to that large face looming against the ceiling and concentrated momentarily. Again there was recognition – and this time there was no questioning whatever: my father in this latest incarnation had been my son in the last. True, he was

---

* As Cardinal Vaughan (1622-95) once observed with distaste

7

appreciably older; I had 'died' before he was thirty and by now he was, I estimated, rather over forty, but it was unmistakeably he. I have never been fond of Gerald as my son, that last time: too priggish by far. Now I would be expected to love him as his son. Of all the unfortunate coincidences. Or was it? Those of us with long experience of The Boss knew well enough of His errant sense of humour: was this whole distressing experience an elaborate device to plug some gap in my maturing? But They wouldn't have left my cumulative memory intact, would they? One had heard of isolated occasions, of course, but they were very rare indeed and, it seemed, usually caused by some genuine oversight or another. Even angels are only angelic: to be invariably infallible demanded divinity.

So Gerald had married that Simpkins wench, after all. At the time my wife and I had died, after that spectacular motorway pile-up, he had been on the point of becoming engaged. We had not, of course, told him of our reservations – what use would it have been? – but now I noticed that the intervening years (fifteen, perhaps?) had brought out the essential hardness which we had foreseen. Well, for weal or woe she was now, technically, my 'mother' and for years to come I would be wholly dependant on her ministrations. I groped around my solar plexus for some kind of appropriate emotion but there was none – only the receding vestiges of that initial shock of recognition.

About the following years I prefer not to be too explicit. I learned to control my eyes, to stop my wayward limbs from wambling aimlessly; to make my voice obey me (though initially it was difficult to remember that I must confine my vocabulary to mum-mum and dad-dad). I learned how to control the excretory needs of my body (a great advance, this) and to walk. Yet, try as I might, there were moments when either through carelessness or sheer devilment I almost gave myself away.

One evening Frieda (I find it most difficult to refer to her as my 'mother') was out at some kind of meeting; both my brothers were out (and I knew where they were and why: they thought, of course, that they could converse safely in front of me) and Gerald was watching TV. For my part, I was playing with some large, lettered blocks which also carried the pictures of prettified animals: by reconstructing the animal you also spelled out the word. As entertainment it left, of course, a hell of a lot to be desired but my owners had decided that the blocks were educational – and also too large for me to get into my mouth and choke on. I thought I would enliven the evening by spelling out whatever four- and even five-letter words were possible with the available bricks. I quickly lined-up three such words, the topics ranging from the scatological to the copulatory, and then wandered over to the toy-cupboard in search of some explosive consonants.

I heard an uncontrollable expression of sheer amazement. Gerald had glanced over at the arrangements I had made, failed to believe what his eyes were telling him, exclaimed (a word which I did not think my priggish son even knew, let alone used) and from a closer viewpoint assured himself that his eyes were really not deceiving him. Clearly, he was nonplussed.

After a few irresolute moments he looked over at me ('Remarkable!') and shuffled the blocks; to avoid any recurrence of the 'coincidence' he then insisted on showing me the boring old illustrations in a book until he could put me to bed. As he was tucking me in for the night, She came home; within seconds She was with us in the nursery. He put his fingers to his lips, motioned to her to go out of the room and followed her, then on the landing outside whispered urgently to her. 'But why are you whispering, darling?' she fluted at him. 'He's only two, you know. You aren't going to tell me you think he understands us?'

She came determinedly back into the room, followed by Gerald. I turned on that innocent expression which (I pride myself) I did so well and soon was caught up in the usual bedtime flurry of hugging and exhortation and 'be a good boy for Mummy.'

The days passed. I thought long and hard about my predicament. Was it or was it not an advantage to start a terrene existence still in full possession of my cumulative memory? It is never comfortable to be out of step in any way with those around you; acting incomprehension, limiting my words and actions, were alike difficult, demanding (like liberty) eternal vigilance.

I saw little of my siblings, who had both been born since my 'decease' and were now into their teens – graceless, clumsy hobbledehoys. They were as little interested in me as I in them – or rather, even less so. There was some interest for me in listening to their conversation when my 'parents' were not present: assignations and their intended consequences, minor shopliftings and the like, more (I think) to demonstrate derring-do than out of any genuine wickedness. There were scurrilous anecdotes about various people as yet unknown to me. For these two I could feel no flicker of affection and I am certain that they felt nothing for me: I existed only on the periphery of their lives. Once they had established that they could not be left to baby-sit with me, we had little social intercourse. I was quite content that it should be so. In view of later developments it was as well that things were as they were.

One day, I remember, I was very bored indeed; She was doing some kind of household chore in the kitchen and I was in the lounge ostensibly amusing myself with the usual 'educational' toys provided for a child rapidly approaching the age of four. With great difficulty I climbed on to the piano-stool and, as well as my pudgy little hands permitted, tried to pick out the notes of 'Fuer Elise' – one of my few party pieces in that earlier existence. It was quite impossible to stretch my hands across a chord and I was reduced to using two index-fingers. That intricate little transitional phrase – you know the one – gave me a great deal of trouble but I was determined to find the sequence. After several attempts I got it right but before I could go on I was seized from behind and held up so that her face could gaze at mine from a distance of no more than some two feet or so. She was bewildered. Then she put me back on to the stool and demanded, 'Play again for Mummy.'

I looked blankly at her, pounded the notes discordantly with two fists and looked at her for approval. Later it was her turn to explain when Gerald came home from work. They went into a huddle, talking in low voices, occasionally glancing at me over a shoulder. I was watching Tom and Jerry, my favourite programme in this as in the earlier existence in this same house, and affected to notice nothing.

But in the future, I resolved, I must be much more careful: I did not want to become some kind of freak (though, of course, that was exactly what I was).

Although I could now toddle about happily enough it had been decided that the stairs were too dangerous for me. Accordingly a small gate slid into slots alongside the bottom stair and upstairs was a forbidden world. I was carried up each evening, placed in my cot and carried down again the following morning but there was absolutely no chance to explore. My explorations were limited to the ground floor. I investigated systematically; there had been many 'improvements' – her taste ran to chintz and pastel colours – but everywhere needed another lick of paint. That last time I had been rather a DIY fanatic but Gerald had not inherited my tastes. The results were now clear to my beady, questioning eyes. I had to admit, though, that the place was clean enough despite the systematic attempts of my siblings to reduce it to muck and misery. I ached for a chance to explore the bedrooms but that infernal gate stood constantly before me as baffling as any drawn sword*.

Then one day, clearly, another decision had been made: the gate was missing. I clambered rapidly and a mite unsteadily to that desired land before anyone could rectify the possible oversight. At the top of the stairs was 'my' window: it looked out over the gardens to the fields beyond and the loom of the distant Brendon Hills. I had always kept that window-seat

* Genesis Ch3 v24

cushioned and in the old days that had been a favourite spot for reading or just sitting. Now, I found, my cushion was gone.

I marched into the nearest bedroom and grabbed a large pillow, tottered over to the window with it and was soon back in that well-loved spot, my back against the wall on one side, though my feet no longer, of course, reached across to the other wall.

There was a startled gasp: Gerald had come quietly up the stairs and found me there as he had so often seen me in past years. His face showed his shock and bewilderment, then he had turned and gone rapidly back down. There had not even been time enough for me to smile at him. His startled voice rose from the kitchen, though I could not quite make out the words, then both of them were standing at the foot of the stairs, gazing up at me. I smiled down at them, babbled something suited to my age, and switched my attention outwards again. The cloud-led shadows were wandering slowly across the grassy face of that distant hill-side; a buzzard sailed in lazy circles; a row of birches twinkled at me in the slight breeze. I had almost forgotten how very beautiful the earth could be and I offered up a spontaneous vote of thanks to The Boss. Somehow I had the impression that He had intercepted it, and was pleased.

On several subsequent days I left a pillow on the window-seat and eventually the message was effective: my original cushion had been retrieved (from the garden shed, as I later found) and awaited me. True, it was decidedly faded and some of the buttons had fallen off, but I greeted it as an old friend; once more, I sat there regularly and often.

At the age of four-and-a-bit I started nursery school. Miss listened to Frieda, who seemed mildly ill at ease, I thought, then smiled brightly at me and tried to reassure herself: 'I'm sure Dudley is going to be as good as gold.'

I could see that She was less than wholly confident about this but She kissed me, said automatically, 'Be a good boy for Mummy,' and left. For the rest of the morning I sat in a corner, watching the other children and the staff (Miss R and one late-teenage helper, female) and coming to certain conclusions about the young of the human race. Several attempts were made to get me to join in the 'fun' but I perfected an unwinking, silent stare which they seemed to find unnerving, so before long I was left alone. From their point of view, at least I was quiet and well-behaved, if in a negative kind of way. Obviously I could hardly make friends of the other children: I had a mental age of forty-nine or so and we had nothing whatever in common. Once or twice, though, I found myself protecting a more-timid child against a pre-school-age raptor – usually in pursuit of a particularly-desirable toy. I heard our two guardians discussing whether I was a nascent bully-boy or just a benevolent protector. When, later, She came to collect me, the air echoed with assurances that I had been perfectly good.

So the days went by and I found what little diversion I could by any means open to me. My interest in the contents of various cupboards was noted but accepted and before long I rediscovered all the books which I had accumulated in my previous existence and was able to while away long hours contentedly enough. ('Look, dear: he's turning over the pages just as if he was reading. Isn't he quaint?'). Often I considered what must be happening in Another Place: by now they must have realised what had happened – surely? What would They do about it? And, just as important, *how* would They do it? In one way or another the process could be most unpleasant. Yet daily routine and the constant cover-up claimed most of my attention and often I forgot for long periods my unique state.

Eventually it was time for me to commence school proper. That first day was so boring – every task I undertook was accomplished at once and automatically: no thought whatever was needed. The class teacher was puzzled: her eyebrows spent a lot of time nudging her hairline. From time to time the Head Teacher was called in to witness but obviously the rule of the game was that under no circumstances must I be given to know that there was anything at all unusual about me. Before long there was comment when it was found that I had smuggled-in the outside sheet of *The Daily Telegraph*, purloined from

Gerald's bag before he left for work that morning. In odd intervals I worked at the crossword and was pleased to find that my old skills, though rusty, were reviving. By the time the paper was taken from me, at morning break, I had filled-in about a third of the larger puzzle; there arose clearly-audible expressions of bewilderment. Of course, it was maintained, my father must have started it, but fancy. A boy of five pretending to do the crossword! Comical, really. And so on. I realised that I must find other means to combat the looming tedium of the next ten or more years. Unless They took some kind of action before then? And if so, what?

It was not long before I was, inevitably, labelled as 'odd'. Members of the staff looked at me with a mixture of expressions: bewilderment, incredulity, fear perhaps, even amusement. For my part, I tried pretty constantly to avoid giving cause for comment but that, as may be imagined, was difficult. I remember episodes when the pressure simply could not be sustained. And still no Hand emerged from the clouds to snatch me up. Would all my knowledge become an asset in the years to come? How could I turn it to advantage? It would be unfair, of course, so perhaps They would send an angel to visit me, to see what could still be done. Yet even They had to work within the immutable rules of the known universe: there must be no overt miracles. Later I realised that I had overlooked the essential nature of terrene time – that device entrusted with the function of stopping everything from happening at once. In eternity, of course, there is no time: Up There . . . but no, I found that I could not formulate an explanation while confined by the straitjacket of words.

Somehow the years went by.

As I have said, sometimes my self-control slipped: my sense of mischief won through the restraints I fought so hard to impose.

In Assembly one morning we came to the stanza about the saints 'casting down their golden crowns around the Glassy Sea.'*

*Hymns Ancient and Modern No 160 Stanza 2

14

I had a sudden vision of that futile activity, of Charlie perhaps still too busy to indulge in a spot of credit-hunting even at that very moment, and I chuckled.

'See me at break, that boy.'

So at break there I was, standing on the Line, face turned in disgrace to the wall, awaiting my turn to enter the Presence.

'And what were you laughing at?'

'Nothing, sir.'

'And do you usually laugh at nothing?'

'No, sir.'

To subsequent futile probings I opposed a resolute silence: had I tried to explain I should quite certainly have found myself in a mental hospital. This squalid little episode terminated in an imposition which had to be done anywhere but at home – obviously.

A year or so later we were sitting quietly one summer afternoon; the sun was shining brilliantly in through the wide-open windows: motes danced in the beams. Outside, the whole sweet day slumbered as we would have done – but for the voice of Miss Dodds. In her portentous way she was relating to us how the Romans had come to Britain, of the relentless march of the legions. Sluggish currents moved slowly in my mind: a picture began to form.

'And on their standard,' she said, 'were three words: 'Victrix . . . ' can anyone tell me the other two?'

'Pia, Fidelis,' I said, almost involuntarily. 'Victrix, Pia, Fidelis.'

I suddenly saw again, smelt again, fresh blood steaming on the cold steel of my sword. Saw again the pile of bodies around the Eagle, still defiantly erect. Now I remembered great patches of an incarnation hitherto buried too deeply in memory.

'Yes,' I mused, more to myself than to the others. 'We were three days' march north of Eboracum on the way to the Wall and the rain hadn't stopped. It was cold, with a chill that soaked into you, right to the bones. How I missed the sun of Apulia, the vine growing against the crumbling wall. It was still another five days before we reached that other Wall. A hundred and ten paces to the minute and five minutes pause at the end of each hour. That day I had the honour of carrying the Eagle, surrounded by the men of my cohort; the previous day I had, they said, distinguished myself in an affray with the local savages and so I had been singled out for that honour.'

I paused, looking through the far wall, feeling, smelling, living it all over again. The room was totally quiet, though indeed I did not heed the others: I was hardly conscious of their presence.

'I was rather concerned about one of my sandals: it showed signs of coming apart – perhaps before the end of that day's march. It would have been shameful to have had to relinquish the Eagle to others and finish the day in the cart with the invalids and the extra baggage. I was looking forward to the evening, I can tell you. Only a ditch, an earth bank and a stockade, but there would be a permanent staff to stand guard, a roof to sleep under, hot food. And I was looking forward to seeing the Wall: I had heard great things of it. We were to be stationed near the eastern end, somewhere near Segedunum, I had heard. My lot, the 7th cohort of the 30th Legion – the Ulpia Victrix – had recently had a spell at Aquae Sulis, from which we had marched to Londinium before we set off north, and gladly. There would be much hunting, so the centurion said – wolves and bear and Picts. Hunting, battle, wine and sleep – what more could a man want? Oh, *that*. Well, I had heard that the local women were not unwilling. And if the Winged Helmets landed in force we would slaughter them and then who knows? Perhaps we would be recalled for a Triumph: across the Rubicon with all our weapons and the crowds in the streets and a parade before Caesar himself. My friend Marcellus had bet me. . . ' Then I realised the time in which I was now living and focussed on this particular present. Around me the other children were quiet and still; Miss Dodds was staring at me with her mouth half-open and on her face a look . . . fear? Surely not. Wonder, perhaps? She closed her mouth (the vision was leaking away

16

and I desperately wanted to call it back) opened it again to say something, knew not what to say and closed it again. I looked down at the floor. The boy in the desk contiguous to mine looked furtively at me and slid away along his seat. Miss Dodds pulled herself together.

'Well,' with an uncertain laugh. 'That was very convincing. Where on earth did you get it all from? Have you been reading a book about it?'

'Yes, miss,' I mumbled. I was grateful for the lifeline she had, unwittingly, offered me.

'You made it sound as if you were there. I'm sure we all enjoyed it very much, didn't we, class?'

Sycophantic murmurs; a few dazed or puzzled looks but I was saved by the bell for morning break.

I realised that I had had a lucky escape: their invincible determination to find a commonplace and rational explanation for every untoward event had saved me. I would really have to be more careful. For the rest of the afternoon I tried to be as unobtrusive as possible but once or twice I saw Miss Dodds looking at me, her brow furrowed in a puzzled frown. At break the other children of the class had gathered in groups but whenever I tried to join myself to one or the other it always broke up in unwonted silence. Indeed, I was obviously so much an outsider that the other children, obedient to a basic instinct, might well have attacked me physically – yet something restrained them. Fear of the Evil Eye, perhaps?

As I left the school that evening, pushing my cycle through the gates, I looked back. Standing at the staffroom window was the Head, flanked on the one side by Miss Dodds and on the other by the woman who took us for handicrafts. There was no need for me to wonder what, or rather, whom, they were discussing.

That night I turned the whole episode over in my mind: *surely* They Up There must know about it? Must realise the dangers inherent in the situation? Must therefore do something to retrieve matters?

17

For a long time there were no more abnormal manifestations. Then one day we were having a Scripture lesson; the teacher, Mr Quayle, prided himself on being open-minded about all matters to do with religion.

'Of course,' he said, earnestly, 'nobody can prove there is a God. It can't be done, can it?' He looked questioningly at us.

I was suddenly hugely impatient at such overt ignorance, imposing itself upon us as authority. I said, 'But sir, there is Saint Jerome's Ontological Proof of the existence of God.'

A startled silence tingled in the room. Behind me someone muttered a comment sotto voce, disparaging no doubt.

Mr Quayle regarded me, clearly baffled. 'Onto . . . Ont . . .' he began. '*What* was that word?'

'Please, sir, ontological. It means reasoning from observation of the natural world.'

'Ah, yes,' he replied. 'Yes. Well, (condescendingly) that may be all very well for the great minds of this world but all the rest of us have to rely on our poor wits.' He smiled conspiratorially at the class. The creeps – the vast majority – smiled back at him in total solidarity; that, they evidently thought, had taken me down a peg.

'But, sir,' protested another voice, evidently unwilling to let things rest at that, 'what about . . .'

'Now open your bibles at page three seven one.' That voice bore down all opposition. 'Chapter Five. Wilkins, you start reading.' So another boring and useless – but comfortably undemanding – lesson ran its course.

Once I had passed the 11+ and gone to the local grammar-school, Scripture was renamed Divinity and once again had me skating around the edge of my supposed mortal limitations. In my second year there the class was engaged in a desultory discussion of a film showing at the local cinema: as at many or even most secondary schools, religion was merely a pretext for anything from social studies to science fiction with an occasional formal nod en passant at the Christian faith. Inevitably the conversation ranged from the Four Horsemen of the Apocalypse to thoughts about the eventual ending of the finite world. There was uninformed talk of Armageddon, of an ice-age, of the world crashing into the sun, the abomination of desolation* (though not even our supposed teacher knew that phrase). It was time I vented my contempt for the sloppy lack of informed thought.

'Of course,' I pointed out, 'you must remember that all eschatology is necessarily apocalyptic though not all apocalyptic is eschatological. If you read Matthew 24 . . . '

'Just a minute, just a minute, just a minute . . . ' An exclamation rung from him and uttered on a dying fall. 'What . . . I mean . . . Eschatology . . . what . . . ?'

His total bafflement hung in the air.

I tried to explain as best I could to his limited comprehension the nature of divine revelation and the number of topics on which it had been known to pronounce. Quite obviously, nobody in the room had even begun to understand me. Fortunately, someone offered a question of mind-boggling stupidity and they were all away, like dogs after a hare. Saved again!

As we all filed out of the room, later, I met a barrage of ribbing, interspersed with a few respectful glances – more, I think, because I had plainly shown up the limits of Sir's knowledge than for my own erudition. All over again I realised that I really must keep my tongue in check†: it could cause me a great deal of trouble. It could also force a situation where They Up There had to take some action to remove me from the scene – and I was beginning to be curious about the long-term possibilities open to me. I could be the most-convincing writer of historical novels that there had ever been, for instance. Universities would fight for my services as a visiting lecturer. Film companies ditto. Yes, the outlook was distinctly promising – so long as I did not put the Authorities on the spot. Over and above that, there were other and unpleasant angles to

* Matthew Ch24 v15
† James, Ch3 v5

19

consider. 'In the country of the blind the one-eyed man is king' – well, perhaps; but in this materialistic age the inspired seer could come to an end as unpleasant as the cesspit which was the fate of poor Jeremiah. (I met him once; a happy soul who had completed his cycle of incarnations and was now awaiting whatever was to follow – and none of us knew what that was, nor would any of the angels snitch.)

Occasional reports of my precocious knowledge filtered back to my 'parents', of course. On more than one occasion She had raised with me some episode where I had been manifestly out of step, not only with the boys of my own age but also with the teaching staff. She would listen to my ingenuous explanation, or endure my sullen silence – and how hard I had to work at each – wrinkle her brow, utter in deepest bewilderment, 'Sometimes I feel you don't really belong to us all.' At least she had got *that* right. Sometimes, too, I would overhear her trying to discuss with Gerald my latest indiscretion, though it was very apparent that he did not want any part of it. 'Kids can be funny,' was about his total contribution to any such attempt at discussing the latest incident.

Time went by – all too slowly, it was true – until one day it was my turn to visit the Careers teacher for the usual preliminary interview. Should I stay on for A levels or should I abandon formal education? A lot depended, of course, on when They would make their play. Or was I, perhaps, intended to be the agent of a new revelation? One way and another, I was totally undecided: at this time I went to bed each evening still weighing all the possibilities.

So I wasn't too surprised, and it was even with some relief, when during one night, just before my fifteenth birthday, I slid slowly awake and realised that the room was full of a soft blue light. I lifted my head from the pillow and turned, and there was an angel standing before the closed curtains of my window. He was six-winged*: an unusual type we did not often get to see in

---

* Isaiah Ch6 v2

20

the Transients territory. The twain with which he covered his face were slightly apart so that he might regard me earnestly; the twain with which he did fly were bent back against the low ceiling of my room and the twain with which he covered his feet seemed to be partly caught-up in the tangle of leads from my music centre. I did not like to draw his attention to it but I hoped that he was aware of the situation before he attempted, later, to do any flying: that music centre had cost my son/old man quite a lot of money and in any case he (the angel) had his dignity to consider. As I sat up he registered the movement and demanded curtly, 'Name?'

'Dudley Pennington,' I replied.

'No, not that one,' he replied wearily, permitting himself the merest soupçon of annoyance. 'Your eternal identity, of course.'

'X371/A/4732/J.'

He consulted briefly a paper which he was holding (with all those various wings, I could not see where his arms were attached though he certainly had hands; it was rather a puzzle).

'You know why I'm here, of course.'

'Of course. I've been wondering for a long time what You were going to do about it. One thing, (defensively) you can't blame me.'

'Nobody's blaming you,' he reassured me. Then thoughtfully, 'If you're curious, the angel i/c Despatch was suspended from duty. Still, that's neither here nor there. We've got to get you back somehow. Can't have you running around like that with all your memories intact. First thing you know, you could find yourself leading a new religion. Too many of them already. Wouldn't be fair on the others, either: they have to believe without hard proof, after all.' Here he paused but before I could get in a word he resumed, 'Expect it will have to be an ACI job. Heaven knows what a post-mortem would establish.'

This time I did manage to interrupt. 'ACI?' I queried.

'Assumed Corporeally Intact,' he explained. 'Like Enoch.'*

* Hebrews Ch11 v5

21

Or, come to that Elijah*. But of course, no fiery chariot: can't afford to have them all gaping up into heaven. Time enough for that when . . . We've got to think of something. You'll be expected to co-operate, naturally.'

He paused for breath and I seized the chance.

'It wasn't my mistake, you must remember, in the first place. Besides, I'm beginning to enjoy the situation. Great advantages, soon at any rate. I'm sure I can figure out a useful angle.'

He looked at me reproachfully.

'Of course, it's your right if you insist,' he pointed out. 'But you could find yourself unpopular when you did eventually get back Home. Future incarnations could be, well, unpleasant. Not revenge, of course: more designed to inculcate a humble state of mind. I'm sure you can think of several possibilities.'

Indeed I could. Easily.

'On the other hand,' he continued, 'if you were to co-operate it could mean promotion, and as to future incarnations, well, currently we're trying to decide on a President of the Pan-European Federation when it will be established early next century. About the year. . .' he paused and withdrew some kind of watch from his robes, '2150. That should give you time for a proper rest before the next time. Well?'

The proposition was tempting, I must admit. And the consequences if I refused to co-operate sounded unpleasant. I could imagine the self-criticism sessions with my Guardian Angel: the thought was enough to raise a heartfelt shudder. So I nodded.

'Right,' he replied. 'I though you might see it our way. Of course The Boss (he genuflected, rather sloppily, I thought) will have to be kept informed. Now as to details.'

He brooded. I was silent, wondering how They were going to work this ACI stunt. Then he started to speak again, slowly; I could see that he was reasoning it out even as he spoke.

* 2 Kings Ch2 v11

22

'It must be made to look like an accident, and there must be no body, afterwards. That means either fire or water.'

He looked at me calculatingly. I shuddered again: neither alternative was to any degree attractive.

'We must think about your two present owners, too,' he pointed out. (Really. 'Owners', indeed.) 'They must be cushioned against the shock of losing you. Yes. Now supposing you dived in off the pier one day, to save a life. We'll arrange a few hefty waves to make it look convincing. At the risk of your own life and all that tosh. You would help him to a lifebelt (we'd better make it a young child: more sympathy that way) but are then ripped away by the currents and the undertow and all that, so that your body would never be found. We'd have you out of there in no time, of course.' He brooded; so did I. 'That ought to make a convincing scenario, don't you think? We could arrange a posthumous award for gallantry so that your owners could be proud of you; there would be a public presentation so that She would have the opportunity to act the brave mum, in public. You know how she'd like that. By way of a more material consideration, we could always approach That Other Place (we do work together from time to time) and arrange for one of their insurance salesmen to call in and get them to take out a whacking great insurance on your life – say, a month before D-day. Your mother would be able to buy that new bungalow she has her eye on and your dad would be able to treat himself to a Porsche at last. Bit late in life for him, I suppose, but better late than never (a thoroughly heretical saying, by the way: encourages procrastination in Good Deeds, I always think). Well, what about it?'

So we assured each other of mutual esteem and he lifted a hand in blessing, then he made preparations for departure. He folded all his wings – quite a business – and rose an inch or two from the floor and started to fade out. The various leads to my hi-fi became momentarily agitated, then there was a faint but vehement expletive, immediately suppressed, and he was gone.

Everything followed according to plan. On the day, I dived

23

into the water, not without some misgivings, but at once found myself at the Arrivals desk. Clearly, I was expected; equally clearly, my co-operation in the manoeuvre had met with general approval. My GA greeted me: 'Back so soon?' but his strained smile, albeit as fleeting and as cold as the fitful gleam of moonlight on a crematorium wall, showed well enough the unwonted effort he was making in the direction of affability. He hurried benevolently through the usual form-filling while I basked in the knowledge that I had the Very Highest Assurance that this time I could look forward to an extended period of what is known below as r and r – rest and recuperation.

It was, I felt, the very least I deserved.

2

So perish all . . .

Extracts from a diary apparently kept by Robert Parkin, lately of 'The Laurels', Herts, and found after his transfer to the Somerston Hospital in September 1985

Trinity 2
External temperature at 7.05 am: 15 degrees Celsius
Relative humidity: 62%
Barometric Pressure: 1034 millibars
Cloud: Five-eighths broken cumulus, moving slowly from south-west at ca. 2,000 feet.
Roads: dry, with early dew now clearing.
Visibility: unlimited

Set off for church as usual. Once again, trouble with the traffic lights at the Pinner Road/Station Road junction. As I approached they showed a reassuring green, though I was on the alert for them to change so that I would have to stop. At a point no more than twenty yards away I decided that it was now safe to speed up a little but at the last possible second, if not even a second too late, the light flicked momentarily through amber and showed a red unwavering glare. I managed to stop, with difficulty, just at the white line. Of course, there was nothing whatever approaching from the other direction: at that early hour (7.28 am) there were very few other cars on the road. I sat there, irritated I must admit, for at least three minutes while the

25

light held me on red and showed an inviting green to non-existent cars coming from the other direction. Only when another vehicle (actually a Post Office van) was about to cross, then the lights behaved just as they had done for me. I heard distinctly the scream of his brakes. The lights held us both for several more seconds, presumably to allow equally non-existent pedestrians to cross, then (reluctantly?) gave me a protracted red-and-amber phase before yielding to green. I drove on.

As I resumed my journey to St Edmund's, I chided myself for my irrational vexation: the thing was, after all, only a gadget programmed by fellow-humans and it was ridiculous of me to feel about it as though it could decide and had purpose.

On the way home later I went as usual by the other route and the two sets of lights which I had to cross, at Pinner Green and at the Ridgeway, gave no cause for complaint. Spent the rest of the day dealing with mail and later, after lunch, visiting friends.

Oddly, I thought about the lights again that evening but told myself I must dismiss them from my mind. With the aid of a bottle of wine and 'Last of the Summer Wine', this I did. To bed.

TRINITY 3

External Temperature at 7.07 am: 14.5 degrees Celsius
Relative humidity: 71%
Barometric Pressure: 1018 millibars
Cloud: Eight-eighths cumulus at ca. 1,000 feet. No visible movement. Slight surface breeze from west.
Roads: Wet, following earlier rain. Shallow puddles in dips. (Must watch braking distances)
Visibility: Unlimited.

As I was getting into the car (7.25 am) suddenly remembered those lights at North Harrow and smiled to myself. Peculiar, how little things like that can bug you. Turned off Roxborough Bridge and wondered what would be the situation when I was first able to see the lights, a mile or so further on.

Once again, I happened to arrive at the critical time, when the lights were just about to change. This time, however, I was better prepared and managed to stop without the drama of last Sunday. Waited patiently, with the merest trace of irritation, for the lights to let me go and finally drove carefully away. I wasn't going to allow myself to be upset by a mere gadget.

Later in the day I found myself thinking from time to time of the junction. I suppose I could use my normal return route for the outward journey as well, thus avoiding *those* lights and using only the two friendly lights – but why should I? Gadgets are there to serve us, not the reverse.

In the afternoon, washed the car and gave it a coat of polish. Must not let this dust get a foothold in the paint. Inspected it carefully for chips in the paintwork but none to be found. I do like my car to be absolutely without blemish.

After some TV, to bed rather earlier than usual. Found it difficult to get to sleep: kept thinking of those lights. Absurd, really: quite lost patience with myself. In the end had to get up, make myself a cup of cocoa and read a few chapters of the current book. Once I returned to bed, fell asleep almost at once.

TRINITY 4

External Temperature at 6.58 am: 17 degrees Celsius
Relative Humidity: 54%
Barometric Pressure: 1036 millibars
Cloud: Nil
Roads: Dry
Visibility: Slight heat-haze.

Once again I was tempted to change my route so as to avoid those lights but I thought, why should I? They are there to serve me, are they not? Why should I go out of my way? It is not as if they are human, surely? So off I went.

And once again, the things played their usual tricks on me – but this time they were just a fraction of a second too late. As the light flicked through amber and to a hostile red I was already almost up to the line and, moreover, in third gear at the full legal maximum. Perhaps even a shade over. At any rate I slammed my right foot hard down and shot across the junction just in front of a car approaching from my left. I looked in my rear-view mirror and saw that baleful red glare behind me and was swept by a sudden feeling of elation: I had asserted myself. What did it think it was? Funny thing, I have a strong impression that one particular pylon, out of the dozen or so at this major junction, is the ring-leader: in some mysterious way it changes from green to amber to red just the merest fraction of a second before the others and they all follow suit as quickly as they can.

Anyway, I arrived at church still with a slight smile on my face and Father John commented on this: I made some non-committal answer. During the sermon I found myself thinking about the light, that particular one, and mentally rehearsed in detail every incident of my victory that morning.

Home, read *The Sunday Telegraph,* did the crossword, got lunch, drove over to Black Park for some walking and generally lazed the day away. At intervals remembered, happily, the events of the morning.

TRINITY 5
External

I have just realised that in the pressure of events today I neglected to make my usual meteorological observations. Still, I have atoned for this by making some others equally significant.

This morning I left home some fifteen minutes earlier than usual, and equipped with a stop-watch. I drove down Pinner Road and as soon as I came in sight of the light I pulled in to the near side, put on the hand-brake and switched-off the engine. The light was, as might be expected, encouraging me with a steady green light. I sat there and watched it: somehow it conveyed the impression that it was becoming progressively more puzzled, more frustrated by my refusal to approach any nearer. Clearly, it recognised me. Anyway, at last it turned reluctantly to a sustained amber and then to red; as soon as it possibly could, it changed back to green in an evident attempt to lure me forward. With my watch I timed it through several cycles and found that it was set for a minute and a quarter on each red or green phase, with ten seconds on the all-red, pedestrian, phase and five seconds on the amber or red-and-amber respectively. So all I had to do was to pull in to the side some fifty yards or so short of the lights, wait until they went into the red phase, wait for one whole minute and a quarter by the sweep-seconds hand of my clock, and then advance to the line, timing the whole operation so that as I arrived the light just had to change to green for me. So this I did and it worked like a charm. The light was obviously rattled and knew it had been out-manoeuvred: it was forced to watch as I motored over the line and away. Somehow, I sensed its frustration.

Ran into Father John as I entered church: he said, 'You are looking very happy these days. You wouldn't like to share the secret, would you?' Obviously, I couldn't: he would have thought me mad. So I made some non-committal reply.

The victory put me in a good mood for the rest of the day. Now I know exactly what to do on all subsequent Sundays.

TRINITY 6

Could hardly wait to try out my system this morning. I pulled-in and parked fifty yards short of the lights, according to plan; then I waited for the lights to turn red and started counting. After one complete minute and fifteen seconds I started the engine and drove forward. The light held on to red until I was practically on the line and then the unexpected happened: a large articulated lorry crossed the junction ahead of me and I had to stop. The light took full advantage of this and maintained the red phase for several more seconds; I could feel its satisfaction that it had triumphed over me, had refuted my calculations. It managed to spin-out its red phase for quite a time – I sat glaring at it, quite forgetting to time it – then contemptuously gave me a green and drew aside to let me pass.

I was so irritated, so angry, that I seriously considered not going to church today; I could go straight home around the next corner (out of sight of the light) and have a large breakfast. But why should I be beaten? There must be some way of asserting my superiority. When Fr John saw me he said, 'You look as if you had lost a pound and gained a penny.' I could only smile weakly: it didn't help at all.

The incident upset my whole Sunday, normally a day I look forward to. In bed that night I was still irritated by it and once again had to get up, make some cocoa, read for a time before there was any chance of getting to sleep. Even when I went back to bed my mind was still hunting over schemes for asserting myself over a presumptuous mere gadget.

TRINITY 7

I should really resume my meteorological observations but have decided to put these off until I have settled this other matter. It is really becoming an obsession: how am I going to defeat those lights – or rather, the ring-leader of them all? If I can defeat him, all the others will fall into line, I am certain. Today I was strongly tempted to forsake the Pinner Road route; but I have used it over twenty years – long before the present set of pylons was installed. I will not be beaten by electronic gadgetry.

Today I had no clear plan of action ready; instead, I thought, I would simply show contempt – it didn't matter to me one way or another whether I had to wait a few more seconds or whether my passage was expedited. Once again the light changed to red even as I approached; of course, I knew this was going to happen and pulled up without any fuss and stopped with my wheels just before the line. Then I switched-off the motor, put on the handbrake and waited. Eventually the light went to green but I just sat there, listening to the car-radio. I didn't even look up: my intention was to demonstrate that I would go when I was good and ready. And at that very second, of course, there was a wild hooting from behind me: another motorist, not realising what was going on, had pulled up close behind me. I made signs to him that he should pull over into the other lane, which he did – and as he went past me he was making violent signs which I pretended not to see. Once he had gone, of course, the light changed back to red. I just sat there fuming.

By the time I arrived at church I was not in a churchly mood; on the spur of the moment I carried on past St Ed's, turned at the next roundabout and came home. All right then: it was a victory for that light. But I would have been in no mood for Holy Communion. Can only hope that I do not have an accident this coming week – after all, why should I? None of it is my fault.

TRINITY 8

Set off this morning with no clear plan of action; somehow, I knew that something would happen. And it did: as I came over Roxborough Bridge a large lorry passed me, heading down for North Harrow. I realised exactly what I had to do: I tucked in close behind him, driving very carefully indeed. The driver knew I was there and tried to scare me off by flicking on his tail lights but I knew what he was up to. On the last bend before the junction I managed to get a quick glimpse down the side of the lorry and the lights were showing green. I knew they wouldn't dare argue with a vehicle as heavy as he was and so I would drive across close behind him – then I would drop back so that They would realise how They had been duped. I had a strong impression that the leader of the lights had a suspicion that there was something going on: almost I felt him leaning over sideways in an attempt to see behind the lorry. In fact, as the lorry's front wheels passed him, he changed instantaneously to amber to red in a despairing attempt to stop me but I was not to be stopped. I must admit that as I shot past, I lifted two fingers of my right hand in a gesture of supreme contempt; in my mirror I witnessed their anger and frustration.

So full of joy and triumph that I made a very good Communion. Veritably, a superb day.

TRINITY 9

Well, the light got its own back today. It must have been thinking all week of last Sunday's defeat, and of my parting gesture, because once again it did its very worst – and I had no plan whatever to deal with it. Almost I had decided to surrender, to use a different route to church, and then something happened which I can only regard as a sign from Heaven.

After just about the longest hold-up of the campaign this far, I got to church and parked the car. As usual I found my pew and knelt down to say my personal prayers but my mind was so full of anger and hatred that prayer was quite impossible. So I got up again. There were still twenty minutes before the service was due to begin – I always feel unhappy if I am not in plenty of time – so I thought I would read the Collect, Epistle and Gospel. In addition to using up the time, it might also succeed in putting me in a better mind for the service.

The Collect was apposite enough: 'Grant us . . . the spirit to think and to do always such things as be rightful'. I would be willing enough there, if only that malevolent pylon would let me. The Epistle was from 1 Cor 10 and seemed to be saying nothing to me until I came to the words 'they are written for our admonition upon whom the ends of the world are come. Wherefore, let him that thinketh he standeth take heed lest he fall.' I felt that tingling at the back of the neck: it was as if the apostle was speaking directly to me. 'Let him that thinketh he standeth take heed lest he fall.' Now I knew what I had to do. I was so excited that I hardly realised that the service had started and my mind alternated throughout between planning the details of the action which Saint Paul had advised me to take and the service proper. When Father John came to the relevant

words in the Epistle I had the impression that he paused momentarily and glanced briefly in my direction.

I spent the rest of the day trying to find things to engage my
mind until I could implement our plan, or at least start to do so,
the following day.

TRINITY 10

Well, it's the great day. Some time ago, my favourite daily
newspaper informed us indignantly of a book which made
available to anyone the method for making and fusing a bomb;
it even gave the title of the book. I am not going to repeat it here
because I didn't agree with people mucking about with explos-
ives, whatever their reasons. With me, of course, it's different:
you could say I'm fighting a battle for humans oppressed by
gadgets. Anyway, I knew of a little shop not far from Charing
Cross station where that kind of book would probably be on
sale – and it was. Then a few calls: one at the garden centre and
another at a chemists, followed by a visit to my local Sainsbury's
and finally to my local Woolies and I had all I needed. I left the
actual preparation as late as possible: the book warned you that
the finished mixture could be unstable. Believe me, I worked
with the greatest of care. Finally I had two small plastic bags and
one timer: I calculated that when one bag went off it would
trigger the other.

So this morning I left home rather earlier than usual and took
a different route: I parked the car just around a corner, no more
than a hundred and fifty yards from the lights. Then I opened
the boot and took out the two bags, stowing one carefully under
each arm; the timer was in my anorak pocket. Then I found out
that I would have to leave the boot lid open until I came back: I
didn't fancy putting down one of my bags until I was ready for
the off. I turned the corner and walked towards the lights. I
could see that the pylon had not recognised me out of the car
and as I approached, it was changing away without a care in the
world. Only when I put one bag carefully up against its base on

the one side and the other on the opposite side did it even show any sign of alarm; then I could see that it was wondering what was going on and suspecting that it boded ill. How right it was. Then I set the timing mechanism and walked quickly away: I should have twenty minutes clear but you can't take any chances in a matter of this kind, can you? Anyway, I walked back to the car, closed the boot lid and stood just on the corner where I could see the fun. The blast shouldn't do any harm at that distance, I calculated, but in any case my car was just around the corner, out of harm's way. As the minutes ticked by I became more and more excited and found myself looking at my watch at shorter and shorter intervals. I will say the timing was spot-on: with fifteen seconds to go there was a loud bang and so much smoke that most of the junction was obscured.

There was the noise of glass falling to the pavements as several shop windows shattered and several burglar alarms were ringing. I felt triumph rising within me. I got back into the car, started the engine and drove quite slowly down towards the lights. The smoke had cleared and a few people, some of them in their night clothes, were already standing here and there, wondering what the hell had happened. As I got closer I saw that the pylon, the ring-leader of them all, was lying flat on the pavement, face down, in token of complete submission; very likely it was dead. All the other lights had ceased working, perhaps out of sympathy for their colleague. There was quite a lot of glass lying in the road and I had to take care how I negotiated the debris. It was probably wiser not to stop for a short gloat so I went on my way.

Father John was just lighting the candles and as usual I was the only other person in the church. He looked at me and observed, 'You look like the cat that swallowed the cream.'

I made some non-committal reply and got down to say my prayers. Should I thank God for my victory? Probably not, so I did not mention it. But the memory of my success carried me through the service and I ignored the sermon totally: I was reliving the explosion and imagining all the Sundays to come when I would be able to travel unimpeded by the malice of my one-time enemy.

But I had no sooner got home from church than two plain-clothes policemen arrived. They had been given the number of my car by someone who had watched me from his bedroom window. Would I please go with them to the police-station, which of course I did.

When they asked me about the explosion I told them frankly that I was responsible. My behaviour, I admitted, had been un-orthodox but had, after all, been for the protection of motorists in general against a gadget which was developing a mind of its own and so causing general annoyance. They expressed no opinion about this; well, I could see that they had to go by the book, whatever they might have thought privately. They explained to me that there were certain things that now had to be done and this I quite understood. They had prepared an accurate statement (I thought it read quite well) and asked me to sign it, which I did. Then it was explained that the following morning I would have to appear before the local magistrate, which seemed reasonable enough.

I couldn't see why I should have to stay the night at the police-station: after all, I was not some kind of criminal, but they pointed out that it was the normal thing so I said oh well, I suppose so. They were very decent, I must say: one of them went back to my place and brought up a couple of books which I asked for and they served up a very acceptable lunch.

That afternoon I had quite a surprise: the door opened and Fr John came in. He looked quite concerned, for some reason. I pointed out that there was nothing to worry about and that I had done nothing wrong, really. He said that the police had suggested to him that I might appreciate a visit from him, and indeed, I did. We chatted for half an hour or so and he promised that he would be in court the following morning. Privately I thought that he was making rather too much fuss about a small matter but he meant well, didn't he? So I told him I would be glad to see him there.

Later I listened to Sunday Half-hour and went to bed: it was a little harder than I was accustomed to, but I relived my moment of triumph that morning and eventually fell asleep, quite contented.

MONDAY, AUGUST

Once again, I have lost track of the date and today I have not been able to buy my usual *Telegraph*; still, I can fill in the date when I get home later in the day. Fancy being able to fill in my diary for a weekday; most unusual.

Went to court about ten o'clock or so and looked around; Fr John was there. I waved to him and he waved back. He still looked worried: poor chap, he must have something on his mind. There were three magistrates and the central one, who did most of the talking, was most considerate. I had seen her before, somewhere, but couldn't recall where. My solicitor (one of my old boys and a close friend) was in court and I was surprised to see him. Anyway there was a lot of talking and I offered to explain my statement but she said there was no need really. After that I didn't pay a lot of attention: couldn't quite make up my mind whether I liked being stuck up there with so many people looking at me or not. In the end it appeared that I had to come back in a fortnight's time and during that time I was to see a certain Mr Powell, a stranger to me. I wondered why but didn't like to ask. One thing: before I left the court it was explained to me that I might go home but must promise not to go near the scene of my triumph. This was rather disappointing, of course: I had been looking forward to going there and enjoying the sight of the, no doubt subdued, traffic lights. I promised and realised later that perhaps they wanted to spare the feelings of the remaining lights.

WEDNESDAY

Today I met Mr Powell; to save me from the effort of driving, he even sent a taxi for me. We had a long chat. He seemed to be most understanding and I explained to him everything which had let up to the incident. He made a lot of notes and showed some sympathy for my position. Finally, after half an hour or so he made me a generous offer: he could understand that I had been under considerable strain and he offered to let me stay for a time – a week or two – at a private rest-home which he knew of, out in the country. If I would agree to this, he was sure he could ensure that the court would approve and no more would be heard of the matter. It was then that I realised that indeed, I had been under a strain and in fact, after a few more minutes I agreed to move in there the very next day.

THURSDAY

The taxi came for me this morning and soon I was on the way to 'The Laurels,' as the place is called. It is very pleasant: quite extensive grounds and surrounded by high hedges so that we enjoy a great deal of privacy. The staff are most helpful and do everything possible to make our stay with them as restful and as pleasant as possible. There seem to be quite a lot of other residents but they all value their privacy and don't make any effort to socialise, which suits me.

I have rather lost track of the days, but today I appeared in court again. The magistrates, the same ones, were reminded of the reason for it all (rather a lot of fuss, I thought); they frowned and then Mr Powell stood up to talk to them. He seemed to be rather mixed-up; he had quite forgotten about me and was talking about someone else, though I couldn't see anyone else who it could have been. I tried to point out that he had evidently mixed-up his notes but was asked not to interfere so I just let them get on with it. He was rabbitting on about 'incipient and progressive paranoia' and I gave up listening; clearly, it didn't concern me. In the end, it appeared, I was released, of course, and my stay at 'The Laurels' was approved. What on earth was that to do with them, I wondered? So back I travelled in Mr Powell's car. He is an interesting conversationalist and we discussed the Georgian poets; he is evidently well-read and we exchanged our favourite quotations. Finally, there I was, back in 'my' room. A couple of weeks, I thought, and I would be a new man.

TRINITY 15

As they explained to me, there is no need to go out to the local church for H C: the priest comes in each Sunday afternoon and we have a short service in the lounge. About four of us attended and three of the staff. Very pleasant but I shall never get used to Rite A. Give me the Prayer Book any day with Rite B as a tolerable substitute.

A funny thing happened this afternoon. I spent an hour or so sitting in the garden; the sun was pleasantly warm and I may even have dozed-off a little. Later I went back into the house and pressed the bell for the lift to take me up to my room on the second floor. The indicator showed that the lift was waiting on the third floor. Anyway, I waited for a time but the lift showed no sign of descending so I pressed the button again. To my surprise the lift then went up to the top floor and waited there for quite a time before repeated pressings of the button caused it to descend slowly to the ground floor. When the door opened it was empty. Some momentary electrical fault, I expect.

TUESDAY

The lift played me up again today: same behaviour as last Sunday. It really is annoying; one expects mere gadgets to function as they were designed to do. Unless of course, . . . but they surely aren't capable of intercommunication? Different species, too. I shall just have to observe carefully.

WEDNESDAY

It is too much. I came here to get away from the contrariness of Things and even here they are determined to thwart my wishes.

Once again today, the lift refused to do as I ordered. I went and found Matron and told her about it. She was most sympathetic and suggested that I told the whole story to Mr Powell when next he visited. In the meantime she advised me to use the stairs. But why should I? Earlier, it will be remembered, I refused to truckle to an earlier wilful contraption by changing my route to church; why should I now have to climb two flights of stairs? In any case, what on earth can the malfunctioning of a lift have to do with him? It would surely make more sense to call in an electrician. Still, I shall do as Matron suggested.

THURSDAY

Matron came around as usual this morning. She seemed a bit on edge. I would like to help if only I knew how. She kept glancing around the room. In answer to her usual query I assured her that I was very comfortable indeed; there was only that lift, of course. She seemed to take it very much to heart and was emphatic that it would be seen to at once. As she left she still seemed to have something on her mind.

This afternoon I went out into the garden for my usual siesta but found that I had forgotten my specs. Went back to my room for them and found one of the orderlies feeling about in my wardrobe. He seemed rather startled; I just looked at him; and he stammered something about checking the furniture. Then he slid all the drawers of my dressing-table in and out but they all seemed to be moving well so he left. Still rather embarrassed, I thought. Really, the standard of care here is superb.

FRIDAY

Funny thing happened in the night. I got up to go to the bathroom; it was 3.17 am. precisely. When I opened the door to the corridor I found that one of the staff was sitting in an armchair just outside my room. I must have looked surprised to see him but he told me that there was always someone on duty during the night and that was as good a place as any. I think he was glad of someone to talk to, for he accompanied me as far as the bathroom door and was still there when I came out again. Really, I find their solicitude quite touching. Anyway, I wished him a courteous goodnight and returned to bed.

This morning Mr Powell arrived and came straight to my room. He asked me about the incidents with the lift and expressed his sympathy. He made notes of all I said and promised that something would be done. Then we talked of other matters; I recited some Swinburne to him and he responded with some Binyon. How good it is to be in touch with a mind that functions much as one's own.

SATURDAY

Apparently I am to go for a drive in the countryside; there is just time to note this before I leave. I expect
There, the bell has just gone; no time to finish this now. Shall see to it when I return.

3

Requiescant

His name was Richard Mason; his age was more years over sixty than he cared to remember; he was a retired schoolmaster and before that, many years before that, he had been a member of aircrew during the whole of the last war. 'Whole', that is, if you included five years of captivity following the day when his light bomber had been shot down not very far from where they now found themselves: driving up the B69, a few miles south of Oldenburg, in northern Germany.

His grandson was driving. Funny, thought the old man: it seems only yesterday that I had to carry him over a busy road. Then there had been all the happy years when their relationship had been so close: driving all over England and, later, the continent. They had even been as far as Africa for one holiday. Such happy years.

The relationship had changed, of course, as the boy grew to stand on his own feet – helped, perhaps, by the security and the confidence that those early years had given him. And now he was driving. 'A time will come,' remembered the old man vaguely, 'when another shall gird thee and lead thee whither thou wouldest not go.' It was not that late yet and with Roman luck it would never come to that.

Amid these musings Mason was conscious of a sign reading 'British Military Cemetery, Sage.' It was barely ten o'clock and their appointment in Oldenburg was not until eleven; plenty of time, therefore. He felt a sudden curiosity; he

41

said, 'Pull in if you can, Des. I'd like to have a look at the cemetery over there.'

There was, as it happened, a patch of open ground a few yards on, next to a filling station and a small hotel: Die Vier Löwen, the old mind registered: The Four Lions. Des pulled over and stopped the motor. In the sudden silence the noise of the radio was intensified. A metallic, female, mock-American voice was wailing:

It's gonna be a stormy night in Alabama,
It's gonna be a stormy night in Alabama,
It's gonna be a stormy night in Alabama –
I guess it's gonna be a stormy night all over the world.

Des punched the button and the racket stopped. Dear God, the man thought: did we really fight and die all those years ago, so many of us, to bring in an age like this? An age of adolescent tastes and standards and values, expressed in vandalism and graffiti, in muggings and burglaries, in endless howls of adolescent sexual frustration? He got out of the car and Des locked it and joined him at the verge of the busy road. Unbroken streams of vehicles raced past in each direction. Des watched both the traffic and the old man and, when a suitable break came, nudged him tactfully and they walked briskly across. Tact, thought Mason, is not exactly a strong trait in his family: perhaps environment does marginally modify heredity. They walked back a few yards and came to the gates, waist high in a neatly-trimmed hedge. Just inside the gates was a massive white stone cross with a sword imposed upon it, point downwards.

'Sage,' read Des, pronouncing it as if it were an English word.

'No,' corrected the old man. 'Sah-guh. You pronounce it as two syllables in German.'

They opened the gate and went in. Spaced evenly across a huge lawn were rows of identical white headstones, gleaming in the summer sun. The far boundary was marked by evenly-spaced poplars, presently some thirty feet high. Their branches swayed slightly in the gentle breeze; the leaves rustled and twinkled. Although the main road was only a few feet away, yet somehow its bustle was strangely muted. The stones were dressed by the right and by the front, evenly spaced in perfect rows; there was a wide centre aisle. At the back was a long, low, brick-built loggia. Mason started to walk along the front row of headstones, his hands clasped behind his back and his head bent slightly forward that he might the better read the legend on each. At once he realised that the whole cemetery was given over to the dead of his own one-time Service, the Royal Air Force. Each stone carried a name and rank, with age and date of death and, at the foot, a simple epitaph chosen by the relatives. The few limpid words failed to conceal the heartbreak. They had been sergeants and squadron leaders; there were one or two simple aircraftmen from the very early days of the war and an occasional officer of higher rank – even a group-captain. And now they lay peaceably side by side in the great equality of death. Once these men had been his friends and colleagues; he had worn a similar uniform and a similar flying brevet; they had met and talked in crew-rooms and Naafis, and on strange airfields. Now they were lined up immaculately, motionless, as if waiting for some ultimate AOC's parade. The old man felt grief welling up into a prayer. He had survived – at a cost: caprice or plan? He would not know yet awhile. One stone, near the back, caused an even greater degree of sorrow: a young man – a boy – barely eighteen, an AC2, untrained in any aircrew trade, had volunteered to man a tail turret in an attack on only the second day of the war and had been killed. Must have been a Wellington of 9 or 149 Squadrons, the old man decided. What call of high adventure had caused the boy to offer? What awful lottery had decided that he should be one of those to pay the price of war so young? But there were many, just as young, later.

Soon he joined Des who was now sitting on the long bench which lined the rear wall of the loggia; there was a roll of honour on the end of a long chain and Des held it out to him. 'Look, Rich,' he said. 'You might even know some of them.'

43

He took the book and slowly turned over the heavy pages: names and ranks, dates of birth and death faced him here, too. Then one name isolated itself from the page before him: Jack Merrick, Sergeant-pilot, and a date in May 1940. D13, said the legend. He stared at it for a second or two: a huge wave of grief threatened to disgrace him. He fought against it and said to the boy – at twenty-one, he was little more – 'D13.' It was all he dared say.

They paced down the rows and found the grave. So here lay all that was left of Jack. He had known that Jack was dead, of course: but in those terrible days so many of his friends were dying that there was hardly time to experience sorrow as each day added its quota to the rising total. Yesterday's dead were soon the vaguest of memories. He had a sudden vision of O-Orange, engines turning, waiting for him. From the pilot's seat Jack waved an indignant thumb; his mouth opened in an inaudible and, no doubt, obscene shout. He himself, burdened with parachute and logbook, trying to run despite his Sidcot and the restraining harness, stumping to the wing-root and scrambling hastily and clumsily up to his hatchway, the rigger passing up his clobber and the undercart safety-hooks. Before he could even clunk the hatch shut the kite was moving, taxying out to join the other two, waiting at the boundary hedge. It must have been one of the last times he ever saw Jack. Some acknowledgement was called for now: he would gladly have stood straight and saluted – he almost did so but the presence of Des restrained him. Theatrical gestures in public were not his style. He stood, for a few minutes, motionless, fighting sorrow, remembering. Then Des, who had been standing patiently behind him, turned to go. The old man took the gentle hint and turned also.

At the gate he wanted – very strongly wanted – to face about, salute, say, 'Good morning, gentlemen.' It would have been only right and proper, the very least tribute he owed his dead friends, but in the presence of Des he was again inhibited. Perhaps if I come back alone some time, he thought. Again Des steered him through the traffic to the car and they got in. Before he had even started the engine, Des automatically punched the button of the radio. A male voice was mouthing:

Ah wanna be some place else, yeah,
Ah wanna be some place else, yeah,
Ah wanna be some place else, yeah,
Yeah, yeah, yeah, yeah, yeah.

Dear God, Mason thought again: how ever did we sink to this level? The car nosed carefully out into the traffic and they were once more cutting their way through the dense stream of vehicles of every description.

The rest of the day passed pleasantly. Their host, the local archivist, was friendly and helpful; representatives of the local newspaper interviewed Mason who had once been shot down in the area and had recently written a book about his experiences. Later the archivist took them to his home for lunch and the two Englishmen passed the remainder of the day eating, drinking and talking contentedly. All over again the old man wondered how ever two such nations had come to fight each other so mercilessly: the inescapable conclusion, which he had long ago accepted, was that the human race was a flawed species, possessing only a modicum of wisdom and of goodness.

Later still they returned to their friends, friends of many years standing, in Osnabrück and a few days afterwards they set out again on the long journey home: four hundred miles to the Channel coast, the usual washboard ride in the Hovercraft and the last hundred miles or so to the western outskirts of London. Throughout the journey, whatever else Mason might be considering, his mind came back to the tranquillity of Sage: the huge sanity of the dead. A resolution formed: he would go back the following year, and this time alone.

A short autumn gave way to a protracted and miserable winter. At all kinds of times, and especially of an evening and during the last few moments before sleep the old man remembered that distant island of peace in a distraught universe. Slowly the months passed. One day, when spring was at last a little more than a mere rumour, Mason went to his cluttered box-room; from under a pile of variegated junk he pulled a battered suitcase and from that he took an old and creased uniform. He bore it off to his bedroom and eyed the three items appraisingly. The passage of the years had inevitably left its mark: a quick trial fitting demonstrated that the stripling which he had once been was now somewhere concealed under several pounds of unwanted and superfluous flesh.

The following day he rolled up tunic and trousers and took them around to the dry cleaner.

'Morning, Chris,' he said. 'Got a job for you. Can you let these out to fit me? It's my old uniform. A couple of inches around the waist should do it.'

Those dark, Mediterranean eyes surveyed the garments; the fingers pulled and probed. The seams were examined. Chris came around to the other side of the counter and unwound his tape-measure. He grunted.

'OK,' he said. 'I fix. You going to a party, perhaps? When you want?'

'No hurry,' answered Mason. 'Some time next week will do fine.'

The following week he collected the garments and in the privacy of his bedroom he tried them on. He inspected himself critically in the long mirror. If you disregarded the face, the general effect was much the same as ever; we used to sneer at Nash, he thought, but I reckon I'm quite as portly now as he was then. But the face – there was written clearly the price of survival. All his dead friends had kept their youth and he alone had paid for the passage of the years. Ah well, he thought, at least they had been good and happy years. I could not have packed more into them. 'To their darlings the gods, the immortal ones, give all things, all.' wrote Goethe. 'All joys (they, the immortal ones), all sorrows (they, the immortal ones): all things.' Well, by that criterion I have been a darling of the gods, he thought. And one day, as in all things, there is a price to pay. Each of us owes God a life: so many of my friends were called upon to repay it early on while I was left to make of it what I could for so much longer. Indeed, I am truly grateful.

He put the uniform on to a hanger and stowed it carefully away at the back of the wardrobe.

Once again it was early July. Again he packed the car – the complete uniform went into a large cardboard box on the back seat – and set out for Dover. First the direct run through to Osnabrück, as always, and the reunion with dear friends. The relationship was as close as it had been ever since they had all met over thirty-five years previously when he, still little more than a very young man, was cycling across Germany on a journey to his last prison camp. Looking back now, with the insight of the years, he could see that at the time he had been trying to assert finally that he was indeed free: free to go into that last miserable hut and free to come out again and go on his way, wherever he wished. He had proved that again and again in the years that followed. Now the welcome was again warm but after only a few days he knew that it was time to move on. After so many years of living alone he was never quite comfortable for long in the company of others. Only being alone was natural and easy and right: loneliness had long ago been accepted.

Again, then, he drove up the B69; he passed the cemetery and pulled on to the car-park of the Vier Löwen. Yes: there was accommodation – Fremdenzimmer said the large sign. He went inside and in his over-precise German booked a room for a few days; he deposited his baggage, had a good lunch and made his way to Oldenburg to spend the afternoon.

The following morning he rose and shaved, then time slipped back forty years: he put on his uniform again. It was shabby, true, but it was neat, clean and pressed. These days, he knew, uniforms were cut of a better cloth than the woolly serge of his day and the tunics were not belted. Yet the brass of his buttons and his belt-buckle shone brightly; the short row of medal-ribbons made a splash of colour against the drab, slaty-blue; the brevet still, somehow, retained the distinction which had once

47

set its wearers apart. No brevets quite like that these days, he thought; he brushed his hair all over again and went downstairs to breakfast.

At the sight of him the landlady's eyes opened rather wider: she had not connected a man of his age with the armed forces. The uniform was familiar to her: men from the nearby aerodrome, both in and out of uniform, often dropped in for a drink or even for the occasional meal. Still, she asked no questions and later the old man left and walked along the verge of the road to those remembered gates.

Again, as in the previous year, it was a day of brilliant sunshine; Mason cast an appraising glance at the sky: good flying weather. Three-tenths cloud; broken cumulus; light south-easterly wind; he remembered. . . and yearned all over again for that lost dimension. He opened the gate and shut it carefully behind him; drew himself up – the older body was not, could not be, as taut as the one it had so insidiously replaced. He saluted very carefully ('Longest way up, shortest way down', he had been taught in his recruit days) and said, aloud, 'Good morning, gentlemen.' Oddly, he did not feel at all embarrassed at so flamboyant a gesture, so strangely out of character for the kind of man he was. There could be no answer – yet he was at once conscious of a welcome, of a sudden calm, as one returning home to the familiar after many years of absence. An aircraft flew over at no great height: he looked up and saw the roundels: an augury, he wondered? No jets in his day, of course: not even the four-engined bombers which were later to become the trade-mark of Bomber Command, as the Spitfire was of Fighter Command. He lowered his gaze and commenced to stroll along the rows, his mind travelling effortlessly back over the years, his imagination recreating a bygone age. Behind him the traffic moved endlessly in both directions yet from here it was no more than a distant irrelevance. A skylark sang in a long, unbroken, rapturous chain; the wind rustled the leaves of the poplars and gently stroked the old man's cheek. 'Lord, it is good for us to be here,' he remembered. Slowly he ambled along the rows of headstones, recreating from the bare details the many who now rested there.

Later he sat in the loggia, gently turning the leaves of the book there, enjoying the undoubted blessing of the sun. Several of the graves had been marked simply 'An unknown British airman.' Their shattered remains had been unidentifiable; impact and fire had down their job so thoroughly. His mind traced a familiar path; somewhere rested the remains of a dear friend, Charley. All over again he recalled Charley's face, his olive skin, his low, soft Scottish voice, his earnest look broken only by the occasional slow smile. He felt again the grief of that day when Charley's aircraft vanished into the distant air; there had never been, then or later, any sign of that aircraft or of its occupants. Somewhere Charley's remains rested in final peace. Slowly it dawned on the old man: any one of these anonymous graves could be Charley's. He lifted his eyes from the page and stared across the headstones, over the hedge, into the infinite spaces of the sky. Charley could even be here.

He put down the book and started all over again his circuit, and as he walked the illogical conviction grew: Charley was here; after so many years (the heartache was long over) they had come together again. The thought brought a strange comfort. Later he went back to the loggia and sat there for another hour or so, dozing at times in that blessed warmth. Then it was time for him to leave. He rose, put the book back carefully into its niche in the rear wall, pulled down the skirts of his tunic (as so often and automatically in the old days), removed and replaced his side-cap and walked down the central aisle to the gate. Here he turned, stood very straight (though not so straight, alas, as did the stripling of those earlier years), saluted very exactly and said, aloud, 'Good morning, gentlemen'. He turned to leave.

As he shut the gate carefully behind him, and quite unnoticed by him, an RAF truck passed. The driver very properly had eyes only for the road and other vehicles; his mate had eyes only for possible talent, as he would name it, and described any passing and nubile female with a wealth of loving and salacious detail. As the truck passed he glimpsed the old man: something odd struck him.

'Hey,' he said, 'D'you see that?'

'See what?' asked his mate, his eyes never leaving the road ahead.

'Just as we passed the cemetery. A WO came out. Oldish. Wore a brevet and medal ribbons. Something odd about his uniform, though.' He brooded for a few seconds. 'I know; he was wearing a belt.'

'A belt? What kind of a belt?'

'It was a belted tunic. One of the old-fashioned kind. My Dad told me about them. He used to wear one. They used to wear breeches and puttees too, in them days,' he added vaguely.

'Wonder who he was?'

'Who who was? Your Dad?'

'No, you berk: the WO' replied his mate, forcefully. Then the topic left his mind, as swiftly and completely as turning off a light. 'What you doing tonight?' he asked.

'Something cheap,' answered the driver. 'I'm broke.'

'Me too. Meet you in the Naafi and give you a run up and down the board. Loser pays for the beer. What about it?'

'All right,' replied the driver, going down through the gears as they approached the guardroom. 'And none of your funny counting this time. You make up the rules as you go along, you do.'

They wrangled amiably about crib and its rules and then as they parked the lorry in the MT section the strange WO was quite forgotten.

That evening in the Naafi, absorbed in their game of crib, they were joined by a crony, a clerk in the Station Orderly Room. In the course of conversation – the usual mixture of scabrous witticisms, pretended insults, shop and local gossip – the story of the strange Warrant Officer was told, mildly embroidered, as is the way of such things. The clerk, a young man of active mind and imagination, whose job did little to satisfy his intellectual needs, showed interest: he dragged out every possible detail.

50

'Tell me again,' he demanded, 'and slowly.'

'Well, we was just passing the War Graves place on the main road and there was this strange WO just coming out. Quite old: brevet – half wing, not a peelo – medal ribbons and the old-style tunic, with a belt, like they used to wear in the war. Never seen him before. Not one of ours, that's for sure.'

And that was all they knew. The clerk was intrigued: the Station was a British island in a German sea and he knew, by sight or by repute, everyone serving there. Such a stranger was in every way a curiosity. The following day he mentioned the story to his immediate superior, a sergeant. That gentleman, however, had other things to think about: half his mind was mulling over the arrangements for the annual AOC's parade, to be held the following week. At the end of the recital, which he had only half-heard, he grunted and asked merely, 'Who told you all this?'

'Perkins, Sarge. You know. Works in the MT Section.'

'Oh, yes. I know him,' said the NCO scornfully. 'Shouldn't pay too much attention to him: doesn't know his arse from a lump of cheese. Probably a Dutchman or someone like that. The uniform's not all that different.'

'Well,' said the clerk, doubtfully, 'he sounded very certain.'

There was a terminal grunt: the interview was over.

As it happened, a few days later that same Perkins and his friend – his oppo, he would have called him – pulled their pick-up on to the forecourt of the Vier Löwen; it was almost midday and they intended to down a beer or two in the idle half-hour before reporting back for lunch. They clumped into the bar and Perkins, the linguist of the two, ordered, 'Zwei Pils, bitte.' It was almost the limit of his German, apart from a few basic words useful in the attainment of his even more basic needs on occasion. Sitting comfortably, conversing but little, both men were startled to see a WO – *their* WO – come into the bar. As he walked past their table he greeted them – they hardly registered the words – then he vanished through the end door. They heard his footsteps on the uncarpeted stairs.

51

'So who the hell's that?' asked Perkins. 'Now you've seen him, what do you think, Alf?'

'Search me,' answered his friend. 'Bloody odd, if you ask me.'

A few minutes later the old man re-entered the room, this time wearing civvies, and entered the restaurant adjoining. The two men gaped at him, looked at each other, rose and left. As they passed the open door of the next room they could see clearly the other man's back: he was eating a good lunch and reading a book propped against an upturned heavy glass ash-tray. Beside his plate was a large goblet of wine.

'Something bloody queer going on,' said Alf. For him the words expressed an extreme of bewilderment. 'He couldn't be some kind of a ghost?'

'Ghost, you drongo,' mocked Perkins. 'We heard him thumping up the bloody stairs. And that was a bloody great glass of wine for a ghost.' He snorted contemptuously. 'A ghost.'

'I still think we ought to report it,' said his mate. 'Could he be some kind of a plant, then? Perhaps they haven't caught up with the change in uniform yet?' He finished on a note of enquiry.

Perkins climbed into the cab and slammed the door decisively. 'That's about as daft as your last idea. This kind of uniform has been around for thirty years. Even the Russkis can't be *that* dim. Anyway, what can you spy on in a cemetery?'

In the intervening days at least two other transport crews had seen the man either entering or leaving the cemetery. To this rhetorical question there could be no answer and the remainder of the journey to the Station there was silence in the cab. As they were alighting, however, Perkins said, 'Well, perhaps we ought to report it to someone.' Alf only grunted but Perkins, who knew him well, recognised it as an affirmative grunt.

Immediately after dinner, therefore, they sought out their friend of the Orderly Room and told him of their new discovery; by now his imagination was thoroughly aroused and he once more buttonholed the sergeant. The latter listened patiently to an account of a WW2 Warrant Officer who was living at the local inn and spending part of his time in the war graves cemetery. At the end of the recital he asked only, 'Are you quite sure about all this? If I tell the Adjutant and there's nothing in it, I shall look a right berk.'

'Quite sure, Sarge,' answered his informant. 'It's jannock. What my Dad used to call pukka gen. Honest.'

'Well, we'll see. Now have you finished those inventories for the check in B4?'

'Almost, Sarge. Have them ready for you by four o'clock,' his clerk assured him.

'Right, then, get on with it. The Queen isn't paying you to stand around here gossipping, you know.'

The conversation was over.

That afternoon the sergeant was chatting to the Adjutant; the latter, a Flight Lieutenant, was having one of his occasional purges when he wanted details of all the functioning of the Orderly Room for which he was nominally responsible. Life was hectic while the purge lasted but by the following week, as they all (including the Adjutant) knew, things would be back to normal: he would sign almost without reading any form completed and put before him by his sergeant-clerk and would confine his visits to his office to the quintessential minimum. As they came to the end of the prepared agenda the Adjutant said, 'Well, that's about the lot. Is there anything else you can think of?'

'Well, sir: have you heard about our strange WO?'

'Which WO? Has one of the old sweats gone round the bend at last?'

'It seems there's a World War WO living at the Vier Löwen. He dresses in an old-style uniform every morning and trots off to the War Graves cemetery. He comes out at midday, gets into civvies and vanishes about his business. Whatever that is. Several of the men have seen him.'

The Adjutant looked enquiringly at his NCO; his eyes narrowed. He knew better than to ask, 'Are you sure?': if this man told him anything, then the information had already been filtered through deep beds of scepticism.

'The Vier Löwen?' he enquired.

'Yessir. Small pub on the main road at Sage. With the gold lions on the sign outside. Some of the men drift in there for an odd drink of an evening.'

There was a little more explanatory detail – not much, for the sergeant knew very little more – then the Adjutant dismissed him and after some thought picked up the phone. He dialled the camp Sick Bay; the MO answered.

'Ah, Bones,' he said. 'I think I have something interesting for you.' He related what he had just been told and the MO, intrigued, arranged to drive over with him the following morning and check for himself.

By ten the following day the two men were pushing open the gate of the cemetery. Ahead of them they could see the back of a uniformed man, strolling among the headstones as a landowner walks comfortably around his estate. As they neared the man he evidently caught the sound of their footsteps on the grass and turned to meet them. A step or two away they stopped. All three men inspected each other, carefully and silently, for a few moments, then the older man smiled. He saluted.

'Good morning,' he said. 'I expect you're wondering who I am: Richard Mason, Royal Air Force, as you see; retired hurt, as they say in cricket.'

The MO's inspection had been professional: sixty-ish, he thought; eyes clear; skin tone good, some signs of facial plastic surgery. The Adjutant for his part, had read the ribbons: Air Crew Europe, he recognised. Now the MO returned the salute. 'My name is Jackson and this is Flight Lieutenant Mathieson. We did come out to see you, yes.'

Manner perfectly relaxed, he noted; eyes steady. No sign of mental or physical abnormality. Uniform very old, remarked the Adjutant: that type went out very soon after the war. Nobody has seen one of those around for, oh, thirty years or so.

Again there was a silence which none seemed eager to break; all three men were now strolling towards the loggia and, having reached it, they sat down in one corner, the WO between the

54

two officers. Mason looked enquiringly from one to the other: they really ought to ask him first, he thought, yet as neither man seemed ready to do so, he offered, 'If you think I'm some kind of a nut, please don't hesitate to tell me. Other people have thought so before and some have said so. Quite rudely, too, at times.' He smiled; it broke the slight tension.

'Well, it is unusual to find you here, and in uniform,' said the Adjutant; the apparent statement was, as they all recognised, a question.

'Yes,' replied Mason. 'I suppose it must be.' He told them of his discovery of the place the previous year, of his wish, then, to return in order to greet his one-time colleagues in a fitting manner. 'There aren't all that many of us left alive these days,' he concluded.

There was a short pause as the two listeners grappled with what they had heard.

'You see,' added Mason, 'the world has altered a lot and often I just don't understand it. I don't understand what I see on the box or read in the papers. I don't understand what people are saying or why they are doing the things they are. When I do understand I generally disapprove. If you had asked us then if we were willing to fight for a world like this, I don't think many of us would have agreed. But here there is peace. I don't think of myself as morbid, but here I *belong*.'

This time there was a long silence; the MO's eyes were still on the old man's face; his colleague looked out over the graves, over the trees and into the far reaches of the infinite sky, its depth only accentuated, that beautiful day, by the few small clouds which wandered slowly across. The MO remembered Koestler's comment on Hillary: 'He thought he came back for fellowship with the living, while already he belonged to the fraternity of the dead.' At least this man was under no such illusion. He said, 'It's getting on for midday: would you be good enough to be my guest at lunch in the Mess? We can talk in comfort.'

'Splendid,' said the WO. 'In my day, of course, I wouldn't have appeared in the Officers' Mess, especially dressed like this.' He looked down momentarily at his coarse serge. 'But I understand things are rather easier these days. It will be good to feel part of the Mob again.' ('Mob'? thought the Adjutant: yesterday's slang, I expect.) They rose and walked back to the gate; here the older man turned round, saluted as usual, uttered his usual greeting. The MO found himself saluting also, though he was silent. They drove back the few miles to the Station; at the gate the corporal SP on duty looked curiously at the strange uniform – he, too, had heard the stories circulating – saluted and raised the bar. The car picked its way through a clutter of buildings and eventually skirted well-kept lawns and flower-beds to draw up before the front door of the Officers' Mess. All three men alighted and the car moved smoothly away.

Over sherries in the ante-room they were joined by several younger men, pilots and navigators for the most part, drawn by curiosity. There were many questions, and a lively and satisfying conversation developed. Mason found himself treated, rather to his amusement, as some kind of a guru. His initial diffidence quickly vanished and he spoke willingly of the old days; the others listened in fascination – this man had fought in the war which to them was only ancient history, the source of their traditions and pride of Service. Each of them had trained hard, and was indeed still training hard, for another war should one ever come about; they had no illusions that it could be won by anyone, yet being prepared to fight it was, paradoxically, the price which must be paid to avert it, if that were still possible.

Later they all moved into the dining-room and sat companionably around one of the long tables; the conversation, Mason was delighted to recognise, was the old familiar mixture of shop, gossip and wisecracks. Later he joined the MO for coffee in a small ante-room; the Adjutant had reluctantly left to attend a conference with his CO. The two men leaned back in deep leather armchairs.

'You must admit,' said the MO, 'That your case is most unusual.'

'Case?' queried Mason. 'Nut-case, perhaps?' He smiled faintly.

The other man answered his smile.

'Unusual: yes, I suppose so. But there is peace there, you know. And somehow, when I'm there with them, I'm suddenly as old again as I was then. I feel that in a way they're still there. Perhaps I am going mad, but it's a pleasant sensation.'

'No, I don't think so,' said the MO. 'I've been watching and listening to you.' He spoke with recognisable professional deliberation. 'You're no more crazy than millions of other people. I could tell you . . . ' His voice trailed away. When it was obvious that he was not going to continue the old man spoke again.

'Back home,' he said, 'I live in an old people's flat. It's very comfortable; in fact, it's the nicest place I have ever lived in. But I'm surrounded by the old and they're a constant reminder. Dust thou art and unto dust shalt thou return, and all that. The thought is less than comfortable. I'm thinking of coming to live at the Vier Löwen. There's a granny flat there which they will let me have at a reasonable rent. I'm good for business: a lot of your people have taken to dropping in of an evening for a drink since I've been there. Besides, I should be there all the year round. At my age I'm not so dependent on people as I used to be. Not even Des.' He brooded shortly. 'But there's all I need here: peace, the company of my old friends, even if they can't talk to me, wine and food, an unspoiled countryside, the sea not far away. Our big cities back home are no cop to live in, you know. It's democracy turned rotten. Graffiti, violence, ugliness, vandalism – many of the people in the flats are frightened to go out at night. Some areas of south London are much worse. All I need – well, almost all I need – I can find here.'

'Of course,' said the MO after a time, 'there's the uniform. You have no right to wear it, you know. Not without specific authorisation.'

'Last month,' replied his guest, 'I was at a dinner where Bomber Harris gave the address. He was wearing full uniform. You often see his picture in the paper and he's always wearing uniform in public. Do you really think he asks for permission each time?'

To this there was no answer: each believed he knew the answer well enough.

'It's the uniform which is the link,' said Mason. '*They* would have recognised it. When I'm with them, it's right that I should wear it.'

Then there was a long silence until the MO looked discreetly at his watch and Mason interpreted the gesture. He rose.

'I'm very grateful to you for my lunch,' he said. 'And for the breath of air, too. Now I must go and change: I wear uniform only in the cemetery. This afternoon I'm off to Oldenburg to have tea with some friends. Perhaps we'll meet again? I've been here a couple of weeks and I'm off home at the week-end. As I said, I haven't yet decided what I shall do.'

They shook hands and parted; a car picked up the WO at the entrance to the Mess and a telephone call alerted the police at the gate. It was all the SP on duty could do to stop himself from saluting as the car slowed; Mason interpreted the half wave as a friendly greeting and returned it. Ten minutes later he was back at the inn.

During the next few months Mason turned the matter over often in his mind and finally reached a decision: he would do nothing until he had once again spent a few weeks at Sage. Yet he felt that at some deep level of consciousness a resolution was slowly forming. The following summer, then, he again took up residence at the Vier Löwen and resumed his earlier routine. Personnel from the Station soon reported his arrival and from then on there were few evenings when he did not have company in the bar if he was in the mood for it. The Adjutant had passed on to another tour of duty elsewhere but the MO was still there and again he invited Mason to be his guest: this time to dinner one evening. Moreover, he let it be known that the members of the Mess expected him to come in uniform. It was a happy time. The Sergeants' Mess also invited him to join them one evening and after a short consultation among the leading members

Mason was put up as an honorary member, with the entree at any time. Somebody at the camp with Press connections even told the story to one of the national dailies, which sent its local stringer for an interview. The meeting might well have been publicised in that newspaper the following morning had not a much-bedded member of the entertainment industry – a 'personality', in the debased English of the day – eloped with a prominent sportsman. The combination of sex and sport, touching two vital nerves, drove all else off the front pages so that 'War Hero Honours Dead Friends' took a very minor place at the bottom of an inside page. Mason was grateful: publicity was the least of his needs. This year he had decided to stay for six whole weeks and the time passed smoothly and pleasantly; throughout, his mind was busy with the question: could this be a regular way of life? What with helping the German gardener at the cemetery on his occasional days off (he, too, was a victim of the war, never having wholly recovered, either physically or psychically, from his four years in Russian prison camps), walking along the seafront at any one of a dozen quiet places, enjoying a modicum of congenial company, reading and the weekly visit to Communion at the Camp – with all this, life was as full as anyone had a right to expect.

On his last evening before his return to England, Mason was sitting, by choice, alone in his small but comfortable granny-flat. He had said his farewells for the year and had arranged several bottles of wine for a final session. The radio was putting out a magnificent performance of Tannhäuser and the music worked with the wine, a magnificent 1976 Leiwener Klostergarten Auslese, to produce a mood of happy acceptance. His mind roamed widely. The magnificence of the Bernese Oberland; the waves breaking on the beach at Scheveningen, driven by a kind of westerly gale; the sky that very evening at sunset – the kind of sky in which Turner would have delighted; the company earlier that evening in the Sergeants' Mess. From that he passed inevitably to the memory of earlier friends – the men who were young when he himself was young. Dear friends,

59

though he had not then counted them as such; he had not, then, consciously savoured his youth or even the very air he breathed. Tony or Johnny or Smudge or Harry, or Ian.

Tony survived, against all the odds, two tours of daylight ops but as soon as the war was over he fell apart, walking inexplicably out on his wife and his parents. He had not been heard of since then: where was Tony? Tramping or dead or in a casual ward or anonymous somewhere in a mental hospital? Johnny crashed on take-off one day: at a hundred feet one overworked engine packed up and the kite dropped like a stone, hit a tree and disintegrated as a thousand pounds of bombs went off. There was no funeral: there had been no bodies. Smudge went straight into the Channel, whose waters were, perhaps, a merciful release from the flames. Harry's aircraft took an explosive shell in the turret; after the wreck had somehow staggered home there was no way to extricate what was left of Harry from the twisted metal struts of the turret. He had to be dismembered. Ian was last seen flying eastwards from Gibraltar, en route for a besieged Malta; somewhere the waters had claimed him and his crew. They that go down to the sea in aircraft and have their business in great waters, these see the works of the Lord and his wonders in the deep.

And there were so many others. Charley Torrance, missing in action after less than three weeks on an operational squadron; Ginger King whose kite crashed, burning, into the friendly earth of Denmark; Tommy, riddled in the skies over Libya. How could he ever remember them all? Yet equally, how could he ever forget? These men had been his friends, he thought with pride. He and they lived the same lives, thought the same thoughts, faced the same fears and gave each other unsparingly of help, support, companionship. And he had survived – at a cost.

Later he found his bed. Sleep was instantaneous, deep and dreamless.

The next day he set off back to England.

During the next few months Mason's resolve hardened even as his distaste for the surroundings of the everyday grew. He would not, he thought, tell his friends – even his nearest and dearest – of his intentions: that would entail too many explanations. So he made his preparations, slowly and methodically.

This final leave-taking was not too difficult, he found. He sorted through his books, his records and his tapes, deciding which constituted the basic minimum. Finally he was left with some thirty or so books (no doubt the number would grow again once he was over there) and about the same number of records and tapes – more of the latter and with a similar expectation. He would need the minimum of clothing, but then he had never been overly dressy; serviceability was the main consideration.

Finally he sat down and composed two very careful letters. The first was to his friend of many years, his executor; he would surely understand. The second was to Des; they had been close, very close, all through that young life but now that Des was married and a father, he had responsibilities enough. These two letters he put carefully aside, to be posted only after he was committed to his long journey.

One beautiful day in early June he packed the car, handed back to the Warden the key of his flat (that last look around, the remembrance of so many happy times, all but destroyed his resolve) and set off for Dover. Before boarding the hovercraft he posted his two letters: the gesture, he felt, was very final. By the evening he was settling-in, contentedly enough, to that cosy flat beside the Vier Löwen, deciding what should go where and like any other old campaigner making himself a simple but comfortable home.

Within days the answer to his first letter arrived; it was understanding, as he had known it would be, and renewed the well-tried friendship of so many years. There was no answer to the second letter: instead, Des (characteristically) came himself.

'But you can't,' he protested. 'Your friends have said how much they will miss you. We need to know that all is going well. We want to muck-in if you need help.' His concern was touching.

61

'I shall be all right,' replied Mason. 'You really mustn't worry about me. I've got all I need here. This morning I had a letter from the War Graves people; the German gardener wants to retire and go back home, and they want to know whether I'll take the job on. Just keeping the lawn tidy and the hedges trimmed and reporting anything else that needs doing. It won't be difficult. If anything goes wrong with me, they'll bring me back to England. Anyway, there are all my RAF friends, just up the road. I shall be all right, honestly. If I want to speak to you I have only to lift the phone. And I'll come over every summer, I promise. In fact, I'll probably get over twice a year; it isn't all that far. Who knows, I might even be able to wangle a flight over to Northolt? – only five minutes away from you by car. So please don't worry.'

Des allowed himself to be reluctantly convinced and the following day he set off to drive back to the Channel coast.

As the car pulled away down the main road he had a brief glimpse in the rear-view mirror of the old man pushing open those gates without a look back.

4

Lone Odyssey

'It may be that the gulfs will wash us down'

Early one morning of a fine Spring day, Man set off for his local railway station. The sun shone brilliantly from a sky almost cloudless and the few patches of deep shadow could not outweigh the golden glow that lay over all created things. It was a day for adventure, for high quests, for the pursuit of joy, and Man – still at that time Young Man – felt the immanent happiness of the day suffuse his very being. Today, he felt, today he would start his journey, a thing he had long contemplated. From the windows of his comfortable and swift-moving coach he would gaze out serenely on the beautiful country-side as it passed before him. Surely, this was the recipe for happiness?

He knew, of course, where he wanted to go and he was not in the least impressed – let alone daunted – by the fact that the majority of his fellow-travellers clearly intended to move in a different direction. The station was busy, its many platforms all crowded with intending passengers. Trains were constantly arriving and departing, often to the cheers of a small crowd who had come to see off a friend on his journey. There would be no crowd to speed Young Man, but this he considered wholly unimportant.

As each train drew in at his platform, Young Man eagerly scanned the destination-boards, but trains suitable for his plans were obviously few and far between. True, there were often local trains which would take him comfortably enough part of the way in his desired direction and he was, at times, almost tempted to settle for less than he had intended. Yet his resolve did not really weaken, even when many of the people around him climbed eagerly enough on to such trains; such people might, he considered, reach the terminus eventually, having travelled a few miles by this train and a few by that, changing all too frequently. No, he thought, such a mode of transport was unworthy of his high, not to say romantic, purpose. He at least would travel happily and securely in the one train and for the whole way. There was ample time yet for such a train to arrive; indeed, he was not short of time: the whole day, or at least most of it, still lay invitingly before him. So he held to his resolve. Where, he wondered happily, would he have reached by the evening?

Trains continued to arrive and depart. Many of them were heading in the wrong direction, though they seemed to be crowded as they pulled out. Some of the trains which were travelling in his direction were too shabby and dirty: better, he considered, wait a little longer for one with cleaner windows, through which he would be better able to enjoy the passing countryside. One had no restaurant-car – and his journey was to be long and he would need refreshment. Some excellent and eminently-suitable trains passed through without stopping: he gazed after them with regret. And there were always trains heading in the wrong direction, but Man would not amend his high purpose merely for the joy of sitting in a comfortable train – knowing that it was not the right one.

At last the very train for which he had waited so long, one which fitted exactly all his requirements, arrived. Hardly believing his luck, utterly happy at last, he boarded it and found his seat. Indeed, it was all he had dreamed it might be; he could not have wished for more. Soon he had even ceased to repeat to himself, almost incredulously, 'At last, at last.' Clearly, he was now committed to a long and happy – even ecstatic – journey towards his desired goal.

And then, tragedy. As the train steamed into yet another station, it was announced that the destination had been changed: Man must alight, must leave his comfortable window-seat, must renounce his happy journeying. He was desolate. Once again he must learn patience, waiting on a platform – far from his original station, it was true – for another train. For this one he had waited long enough and now the day was half done. Well, he must count himself fortunate to have come this far so happily but he felt the tug at his heart as his train – at least, it had been his train until now – steamed out.

At this half-way station there seemed to be fewer trains passing through than had been the case so many hours ago, at the start of his journey. Once again there were passable trains going in the wrong direction or unsuitable trains heading in the right direction, or even the eminently-desirable trains which, however, did not stop. Almost, Man felt his high ideals crumbling: surely, to be travelling in the right direction, even if only in a train which would take him no more than part of the way, would be better than standing alone on a barren platform waiting, just waiting? And in fact, at last – it was by now mid-afternoon – he did board one such train. This train could not take him to his destination, that he knew: sooner or later he would have once again to alight. But at least he would be travelling, on the inside and looking out; and indeed, the travelling was as happy as it had been earlier – even with an added quality deriving from the full ripeness of the early-evening sun painting the whole passing landscape with its unique and precious tint of gold. Once again, he was totally happy. Against his recurrent qualms – this happiness was inevitably limited – he set the idea that this part of his journey might even take him far enough for his new purpose: to somewhere far along the way, a place distant enough for him to renounce the lure of endless travel and simply look around him. Yet he knew that he was only trying to deceive himself: he would have had this stage last for ever – or as near to 'for ever' as is given to humans. Each station that they passed represented sheer gain and the knowledge that this happiness was evanescent lent a peculiar glamour to the time.

All too soon the train slowed for yet another station and this one, it seemed, was the last for Man: henceforth the train would turn aside into regions which were not for him.

This new isolation, however hurtful, could not be as grievous as the earlier one: at least, this time he had known from the beginning that the happiness was to be of limited duration. And now the eager visionary of the morning had become a realist; as is the way of things, the idealist had transmuted into the cynic. As he looked around this third station he realised that the darkness was now not so far away and that there would be no more trains. It was a time when all sensible travellers had reached, or were well on the way to, their destinations. He would gladly, now, have settled for many of the trains which he had spurned earlier in the day, but the chance was gone. Wer will nicht wenn er kann, wird nicht können wenn er will, as the saying went: chance is a fine thing so make the most of it.

Twilight was now rapidly deepening and though the countryside was still beautiful, yet the air was becoming chill. Suddenly Man felt his aloneness: it was time to find compensations. He sought out the waiting-room: not grand, it was true, but quite serviceable for his needs. From his luggage he took books, a radio, even a bottle of wine. He had always valued quiet and privacy and now he would have both in full measure (he suppressed the thought, perhaps even to excess). He philosophised: after all, if my plans had succeeded, if I had journeyed on as far as one can, and alighted at the other end, what would there have been? Why, books and music and wine. And privacy, exactly as here. Even expecting to find a train which would meet all his fanciful requirements was, he saw now, mere youthful romanticism. Amending an old saying, he understood that to travel hopefully was indeed better than to arrive: arrival was static, travelling hopefully, ecstatic. Yet perhaps, to have taught himself to have been content where he originally was and with what he originally had – would not that have been the best of all? As the Romans told each other, oh, so long ago: coeli non anima mutant qui trans mare currunt. Freely translated: travelling gets you nowhere: in the end you must learn to live with yourself and you can, by implication, do that as easily (or otherwise) in one place as another.

So, as the day gradually faded even more and final darkness was not all that far away, he learned the greatest, and perhaps the hardest lesson: contentment.

5

O wad some Pow'r . . .

Although the canteen clock showed four o'clock, the room was full. It was long after the debris of lunch, which the Works personnel knew as 'dinner', had been cleared away and it would be another couple of hours or so before the cast of 'My Fair Lady' would gather there for one of the last rehearsals before the opening night, a bare fortnight ahead. Yet the air was blue with tobacco smoke and every chair was occupied; the buzz of many conversations was unremitting. It was noticeable that Staff, mostly men in dark suits and wearing tasteful ties, had assembled spontaneously down one side of the room and Works, men in overalls or with sleeves rolled up to display ornate tattoos, down the other. Female personnel were somehow dressed fittingly: you could have told at a glance in which classification any of the women belonged. On the table in front of each person present stood a glass: for the men, mainly beer, and for the women, wine.

Over the stage was the logo of the firm: an abtruse monogram imposed on a mock-heraldic shield. The curtains were drawn back and dead centre was a table, lit by overhead spots, over which had been flung a green cloth. To add a festive note, a garish paper-chain had been looped across the front.

Through the doorway at the back of the stage five people started to emerge; firstly an obvious foreman – elderly, rapidly balding, wearing a cleanish overall and a nervous smile; then an equally-obvious office-manager; blue-suited, dark tie bearing the identical logo to that above the stage, frowning slightly at the impact of the powerful lights; thirdly, an elderly hybrid, male, in his fifties, wearing a suit in which he was plainly hardly at ease; after a short interval – some ten seconds or so – a Junoesque woman, neatly and tastefully dressed, smiling, peering through the the glare and the smoke at the assembly before her, accompanied, lastly, by a tallish man with obvious presence and expensively dressed. His gold wristwatch caught the lights as did some kind of stone in his tiepin: the Managing Director, as everyone knew; indeed, it would have been a gross case of lèse-majesté not to have recognised him as such.

As this company assembled the buzz died gradually away; there was an attempt at sporadic applause as the crowd glimpsed the woman among her entourage but it was not taken up and those clapping soon desisted, bashfully. As the MD took his seat with the others, behind the table, the hush was absolute. With some sense of occasion, many of those present put out their cigarettes.

For a few moments the five people on the platform came to some kind of last minute agreement, then the elderly hybrid rose to speak. An anonymous voice at the back of the room called out, 'Good old Sid,' which evoked a titter, although it was confined to one side of the room. Sid himself frowned then recalled the smile which had hitherto been fixed to his face, cleared his throat and began what was quite clearly a prepared address.

'Ladies and gentlemen,' he began. 'Friends.' Having thus recognised the reality of the division in the ranks before him, he launched out with some confidence. 'As you all know, we are here today to wish Godspeed to one of our honoured colleagues who is about to retire. You all know me ('We do that, Sid' – renewed frown and reproachful stare from the MD) and you know that I'm a plain man. You won't get no old clishes from me: what I say, I mean. Miss Wotherspoon, or as most of us call her, Our Enid, has worked long and hard here with us; she has always been a loyal comrade, ready to help anyone, and now she feels that it is time for her to devote her days to doing the things which *she* wants to do. Of course, we shall miss her.' Here he turned to the woman on his left and looking down at her resumed. 'We all wish you a long and happy retirement and we would be glad to know from time to time how you are getting on. To show our appreciation we have held a little collection and it is a mark of what we all feel about you, Enid (if I may call you that on this happy occasion), that I am able to present you with this cheque for no less than two hundred and fifty pounds and we hope that you will use it to treat yourself to something which you very much want.'

Miss Wotherspoon stood and faced him; he held out a cheque with his left hand while they shook hands with the right. There were cries of 'Hold it,' causing them to maintain both the handclasp and the fixed smile as they both looked over their shoulders for the benefit of various photographers. The ensuing clicking and flashing lasted some twenty seconds, during which the smiles became more of a rictus, and then they were permitted to sit down again.

This time the applause was fervent and accompanied by some foot-stamping – from one side of the room; the people on the platform smiled approvingly. Then it was the turn of the MD; as he rose there was an instantaneous and respectful silence. A man who had hitherto been lurking in the semi-darkness at the back of the stage now came forward and placed a large box, wrapped in coloured paper and tied with extravagant ribbon, on the table; then he scuttled back gratefully into the obscurity from which he had emerged.

'Well, you all know why we are here today and I must say I am impressed by the size of your parting gift to Miss . . . Miss (he glanced furtively at a paper which had been pushed across the table) ah, Miss Wotherspoon. The Board also feel that this is a sad day for our team but of course our honoured colleague has earned her retirement'. Now he, too, turned and looked down at the woman, who looked up at him. 'On behalf of the Board, I, too, wish you a long and happy retirement. Any time that you

70

find yourself near us, do come in and renew old friendships. And now I have the honour to present you with this token of our very high esteem.'

He reached down and tugged at the ribbon which, heedless of what was expected of it, refused to come apart. The MD frowned – he was obviously unaccustomed to being thwarted in any matter, however trivial. One of the other men leaned across and gave the ribbon a mighty tug; it fell apart and the MD was now able to remove the lid of the box thus revealed. The front side fell and a most-handsome clock was visible. There was a shining plaque, the message on which was read aloud for the benefit of the audience.

'To Miss Enid Wotherspoon from the Board of Managers, in recognition of her thirty-three years of loyal and capable service.'

Once again there was clapping accompanied by some cheering and stamping. Now Miss Wotherspoon rose to her feet; she dabbed fleetingly at her eyes with the daintiest of hankies – a gesture watched with approval by her audience.

'Ladies and gentlemen. There is not a lot that I can say. I have always enjoyed my work here, as most of you know, and I shall miss you all. I must thank you all and the Board for my magnificent presents. I don't know yet what I shall buy with the money but I shall write and let you know when the time comes. Once again, my very hearty thanks.'

Then, just in time, she sat down. There was applause; at the back of the room there was an attempt to start a chorus of 'For she's a jolly good fellow,' but the voices trailed off and died, leaving humorists digging each other in the ribs to conceal their embarrassment. The platform party looked enquiringly at each other; there was a concerted nod and, led by the MD, they left the room.

The audience ceased to applaud as the foreman – works manager? – turned in the very act of leaving, raised one hand for silence and announced, 'There is no need for anyone to clock-off tonight. The Accounts department have been instructed to credit everyone with the normal finishing-time.'

This, of course, produced approving noises and even some clapping: a present of three-quarters of an hour was unusual enough to be highly appreciated. Quickly the room emptied.

For another ten minutes or so the platform party gathered in the general office while sherry was handed around and platitudes were exchanged. Then the MD signalled the end of the proceedings by wishing them all goodnight and leaving; in another few minutes the party had dispersed.

With a last kiss and a last, lingering handshake, Miss Wotherspoon made her way slowly back to her office; she carried her clock in its colourful wrappings very carefully before her and, having reached her room – up to that day, at any rate, her room – she placed her parcel on the desk. She realised that she was reluctant to leave, to make final the break after so many years. She had been the first woman promoted to Senior Management and so entitled to an office on the third floor; since then, two other women had also been promoted to that level – which could only mean, surely, that her own appointment had been accounted a success? A long time ago, it was true, she had even dreamed of the ultimate accolade: an office on the fourth, top, floor, reserved for Top Management. Ordinary mortals, even at her level, were by an unwritten law expected never to set foot upon those deeply-carpeted corridors. But that last step had never come about and she had long since given up regretting her partial failure, as she had once considered it. Now, however, was her chance: everybody would by now have left the building and a short journey of exploration would not be noticed. She entered a lift and guiltily pressed the button marked, in bright red, 4. The door opened and there was the forbidden land stretching before her: a corridor much like her own, one floor below, but with fewer doors (the offices must be larger?) and the carpet, once she had set foot on it, was of a depth and softness as were not to be found anywhere else in the building. She walked slowly along, enjoying the guilty thrill of being in prohibited territory, enjoying the subdued lighting, the delicate colours. Then behind her she heard the clang of a pail: heavens, the cleaners! But there was another lift at the far end and so the cleaners need not see her, though even if they had done so, there was nothing they could do about it more drastic than to report the matter on the following Monday. By then, of course . . . Yet even now she did not want to mar the blameless record of some – could it really be thirty-three years? And at just that moment she realised that she was about to pass before an open door, that there was a gleam of light on the wall inside, and that a man's voice had just pronounced her name. Considerably confused, she stopped and froze.

'Poor Enid,' said the voice. 'A good sort, really. Lots of people will miss her, right enough, but none of them up here. When we first appointed her – you weren't with us then, were you? – she was as good as any of the other possibilities. And Women's Lib was just beginning to make itself felt so we thought it would be wise to have a woman in Senior Management for the first time. For the first few years it all went well and we congratulated ourselves on our choice but slowly, very slowly, it all began to change. There have been enormous developments in our line of country over the last ten years, as you know; don't understand some of the gadgetry myself. But as the head of R and D she ought to have kept herself abreast of new possibilities. Gradually her department became less of a little ball of fire. I used to drop various technical magazines on her table with certain passages marked but she never took the hint. Always thanked me, of course, and meant it, but the penny never dropped. Five years ago we pointed out that if she would care to rest on her oars we would think of a suitable handshake, not gold, of course, but at least cupro-nickel. Would have been quite generous. But she only thanked us for our generosity and said she couldn't take advantage of us like that. And you could never get her to sack anyone: said she couldn't bring herself to do it, brought up all the background – invalid mothers and all that crap. So she gathered all the no-hopers around her. There was never any one thing to which we could have objected enough to force her out and if we had just gone ahead we would have had the Equal Opportunities Commission on our necks. That kind of publicity we can do without. The buyers we have to deal with are usually women and there's nothing like female solidarity if they think one of them is being ill-used.' There was a pause, the sound as of a carafe tinkling against a tumbler, repeated, a long-drawn sigh as of someone drawing on a cigar.

Miss Wotherspoon stood motionless, her mind seething with emotions. She ought not to be there. She ought not to have listened but then if she crossed that part-open door she might be visible to the men in the room. Now that she must have overheard their conversation, the thought of being detected by them would be even more embarrassing. Should she turn and dare the reproachful glances of the cleaners? The voice started again.

'There was one thing she was insistent about: of all people, *you* must not take over the department. I think she was afraid you would root out all her protégées. So we didn't tell her who would take over: said we would leave her deputy to run the thing on a temporary basis. Give yourself a month and see whether any of them pull their socks up – timekeeping, excessive days off and so on – then do whatever you think best. There will have to be some blood-letting, of course, but as I said, give it a chance to settle down and then do whatever has to be done. We'll support you.'

'Thank you,' replied another (male) voice, one which Miss Wotherspoon knew only too well. She really could not wait for more: whether she was seen or not, she just had to escape.

Tears were running down her face, tears of rage and hatred for them all. All those things they had said to her face and now this, behind her back! What they must have said to each other on many other occasions: it was humiliating.

She scuttled desperately past that open door; out of the corner of her eye she could see that whoever was in the room was not visible from her viewpoint. In that deep pile her feet were soundless, and then she was in the lift, pressing the button for familiar and rightful territory. And still the tears ran, quite beyond her control whatever she might do.

Then she was back in her room, looking around helplessly, and suddenly aware of that box on the table. She felt a sudden wish to raise it above her head and smash it down on to the floor as hard as she could – but the noise might bring one of the cleaners. She went over to a cupboard in the corner; on the top shelf were many old ledgers, mute survivors of the earliest days of the firm and intended for a permanent display once someone got around to setting it up. It had even been suggested, once, that she herself might undertake the job . . . Roughly, she bundled several of the books down on to the table, leaving a space at the back; two of the tomes thumped to the carpet but she ignored them – indeed, it was doubtful whether she was fully aware that they had fallen. Now she pushed the envelope with the cheque into the box beside the clock and pushed the box to the very back of that top shelf. Then she replaced the ledgers; in all probability, nobody would have cause to disturb them again for, oh, years to come.

And still she was weeping, tears gathering at her chin and falling; occasionally she dabbed at them in a futile kind of way. After all those speeches! Lies, barefaced lies. And she had believed them. How they must be laughing at her. 'Do come in and renew old friendships.' As if!

She put on her coat – for the last time in this place. Then the lift took her down to the entrance lobby. As she emerged and made for the front door two of the typists from the Pool were just on their way out.

'Goodnight, Miss Wotherspoon,' they chorussed, but she did not, could not, answer. Face set, the final tears still visible on her cheeks, she headed determinedly for the front door. She passed George, the security guard, in his little cubicle; he, too, greeted her and he, too, was ignored. Then the front door opened, letting in momentarily the roar of the rush-hour traffic outside, and slid gently shut again.

The two girls looked at each other and then at George. 'Catch me crying just because I was leaving this dump,' said one.

'And with a clock and a hefty present and a pension,' added the other. They nodded to George who half-waved and once again the door opened, the roar of traffic disturbed the silence and was cut off again.

George watched them go then unfolded his paper and settled down in front of his little electric fire. Women, he thought.

6

' . . . that's for remembrance.'

Of course, you would find it hard to believe, now, but in my younger days I was much fancied – by men as well as by women. Quite good-looking, I was. The trouble was that in those days I wasn't ready for loving and all that caper – not from either side, if you see what I mean. I found a photo the other day, of me and my friends back on the squadron, in 1940; we were all about the same age, eighteen or a bit over – only children, really – and it's amazing how clean-cut and unused and just plain boyish I looked. I could almost fancy the me I then was, if that's not an immoral suggestion. In those days, I remember clearly, I was utterly happy, utterly carefree: life gave me in full measure all that I wanted, then, and all I wanted was my job, flying, and the company of my mates. As I said, I hadn't a care in the world. From time to time someone showed that kind of interest in me – you know – but I was always off like a scalded cat, whether it was a man or a woman. I didn't really understand what it was all about but instinct told me to avoid any unnecessary complications.

Not long after the war broke out, a new sergeant joined the Section. He had been serving at Shaiba – the RAF's least-popular posting – and seemed a decent enough chap. His name was Lee, Peter Lee, and within a very short time it was obvious to all of us that he was paying rather more attention to me than mere duty warranted. I don't know whether his needs were inherent or whether they had been brought out by conditions

77

down the Gulf – bit of both, perhaps. It wasn't long before the comment started.

'See you got a new mate,' said Ian, artlessly, as we strolled up to the cookhouse for dinner one day.

'Oh?' I answered in all innocence. 'Who's that, then?'

'Peter, of course,' he replied. 'I hear he's putting you forward for the Order of the Golden Rivet.'

There was only one answer to this so I thumped him, hard.

There might have been a very promising fracas then but we had to pack it in to salute a couple of officers coming the other way. By the time we reached the cookhouse the conversation had, mercifully, taken a different turn. But the topic returned that evening, back in the billet. The others, a mixed bunch of tradesmen, were out to make the most of my embarrassment. In the end I shut up and waited for the topic to die a natural death; once I made it obvious that the joke was over the others soon got to discussing the ever-burning topic of how to recognise a nymphomaniac if you were ever fortunate enough to meet one. For the moment I was off the hook. A couple of evenings later, however, the whole section turned out for another evening at the King's Head: it was effectively a three-line-whip occasion, to welcome Peter officially to the Station.

Later we walked back up the road to the Station, between the two high hedges. There was a full moon, which, perhaps, exacerbated Pete's amatory needs: I realised, too late, that he and I were walking a hundred yards or so behind the rest of the gang. It was only later that I realised that they had plotted this and had surreptitiously cracked on speed and left us. I tried to quicken the pace, to catch up with the others, but Pete seemed well content to amble along behind. I was most apprehensive what he might say, what overtures he might make: I wouldn't have known how to give him the brush-off. After all, he *was* a sergeant and could have been quite unpleasant during working hours. If he had wanted to, of course. But he didn't say anything – though he did look at me sometimes. Mocking?

Inviting? Assessing? I was not experienced enough to know.

Eventually we got back to the billet.

'Call yourself mates?' I asked, bitterly. 'Did your best to drop me in the shit, didn't you?'

There was a roar of laughter; several people spoke at once.

The intention had been to enjoy my reaction and the others agreed that the ploy had been a huge success. I could not share their amusement.

From time to time Pete caught my eye in the Section but I perfected a blank stare and ensured that I was never in there alone with him, so that he could never speak freely – if indeed that was his intention. I wasn't shocked or angry or anything of that kind: I just didn't *want*.

It wasn't long after the night of the booze-up that the Squadron started to take quite heavy losses. Ian was in a kite sent to bomb shipping off the Norwegian coast and they never came back. Several other aircraft were lost in the course of senseless attacks on targets all over northern Europe, and one of my friends was lost each time with his kite. Then Pete himself went; the aircraft in which he was flying was last seen on fire, diving steeply into the sea. Perhaps he was already dead before the water reached up to douse the flames. I had one or two nasty moments myself, and could hardly deceive myself about my own chances. 'Those whom the gods love die young,' said the ancient Romans and perhaps they were right; my friends are still fresh, young, carefree in my memory while I . . .

Anyway, I stopped going to the King's Head – you couldn't help remembering your mates who would never share a drink there with you again – and that's really how I met Vic.

That Saturday evening I had declined the invitations, the offers of free beer, the friendly jibes, the appeals to Section solidarity: I watched the others – a few, too pitifully few, of the old gang among them – tidy themselves up and leave for Ramsey. I had a couple of letters to write and afterwards, I thought, I would get some supper at the Naafi. There was plenty at the cookhouse – as much as you wanted, in fact, but

79

the thought of bread pudding made from left-overs, bread and cheese and cocoa, was not appealing. I was thinking along the lines of a proper meal: food rationing had not then bitten very deeply and you could still get a meal almost as good as the one you could enjoy before the war had started. Followed, of course, by the obligatory char-and-a-wad. When I got to the Naafi there were very few people there and they were scattered over the huge room; mostly, I noticed, they were duty-men: fire picquet, guard, duty flight, and they all had to be back at their posts after the shortest possible break. I went over the the counter to order. Instead of the usual manageress we had a manager, a youngish chap from Nottingham. He seemed pleasant but didn't gossip much; we approved of his efforts to keep the girls on their toes – since his advent the tables were much cleaner and constantly kept clear of dirty crockery and over-full ashtrays. This evening Vic seemed to be alone behind the counter; he took my order and passed it through the hatch to the cook, then came back to pour my tea.

'All alone tonight?' he asked.

'Yep,' I replied. I explained that I hadn't wanted to spend the evening in a pub.

'Tell you what,' he proposed. 'Why not come through and have your supper in my room? We could have a natter. There's a lot I'd like to ask you about flying.'

The chance to talk about kites and flying – the next best thing to actually flying – was hardly to be refused and it was flattering to be offered preferential treatment. He lifted the flap of the counter and after a quick look around – most of the duty men seemed to have gone – I went through. He quickly laid the table in his small living-room, part of his private flat, and we had a civilised meal together, broken only when the infrequent airman turned up for attention. It was a pleasant change to eat at a proper table, with a real white cloth and decent crockery and cutlery. Our conversation was chiefly on the lines of question and answer: he asked all the questions and I supplied all the answers. It gratified my self-esteem to become an instant expert. He wanted to know about the sensations of flying, the feeling of being in action ('Simple, chum: I'm always shit-scared'), our general approach to life. He asked about several of my friends, describing them so accurately that I could name them, and was saddened to hear that some of the people he had been observing would never appear in his canteen again. He would, he told me, gladly have joined us but an attempt to do so had resulted in his rejection on the grounds of a heart murmur.

It was almost two hours that I spent in there; the shutters had long since been run down and for a whole hour we had not been disturbed. Once his curiosity about flying matters had been satisfied, I asked him the few questions that occurred to me. He was, it seemed, twenty-four; having failed to get into the RAF he had joined Naafi so that at least he might be useful to airmen. Both his parents were dead; I did not pry into that. He was of medium height with nondescript hair and features that dissolved easily and often into a friendly grin, not much in evidence when he was on duty. Eventually our conversation flickered out and we sat in an easy silence, half-listening to the radio, passing the odd comment. He was, I discovered, well-read in the tragedies and the sonnets of Shakespeare; he had some kind of acquaintance with the historical plays but no time at all for the comedies. Indeed, he had a theory, at least half-serious, that the name Shakespeare concealed at least two writers and perhaps more, and that the author of the comedies had confined himself to those alone. Sometimes he quoted odd scraps – mostly, I think, from Hamlet. My own two set books, in two consecutive years, had been the Merchant and Macbeth; in deference to his views I did not mention the former and expressed a modified appreciation of the second. Yet I was able, once, to catch him out in a misquotation. Apropos of something or other, he said, 'There's roses: they're for remembrance.' 'Stop,' I said. 'I'm sure that's not right. Isn't it . . . isn't it rosemary?'

He thought briefly. He smiled engagingly. He admitted, 'Yes, you're right. But roses would be nicer, wouldn't they?'

It was the only time I ever caught him out and even then it was the merest fluke on my part. Perhaps that is why I remembered it so clearly afterwards, when . . .

As I was leaving I said, 'Well, thank you for a pleasant evening. See you tomorrow, I expect.'

'I've enjoyed it, too,' he answered. 'I always wanted to know about flying. I'll have a lot to think about. Tell you what: if you let me know what you would like, I'll lay on supper specially for you next Saturday. What about it?'

It was flattering to be treated as someone special as, in his eyes, I clearly was. I thought briefly: undoubtedly next Saturday evening the others, or the survivors, would be off down to the pub again and I would once again stay in camp. I said, 'I'm very fond of sea-food. Crab, perhaps?'

'You're on,' he answered immediately. 'Crab salad. Next Saturday, then. Eight thirty?'

'Eight thirty,' I confirmed.

And that was how it all began. Curiously, this time the alarm bells did not ring. Of course, I soon began to realise that his interest in me was, well, less than (or do I mean more than?) just friendly. Yet it became an understood thing that every Saturday evening I would drop in for supper. It was a civilised interval in the week. I quite liked him, he never in any way even sounded as if he was on the verge of a proposition – and the food was free. No small consideration when my daily pay was less than five shillings: trade, gunner's and crew pay combined. Again, it was pleasing to be valued: it was plain that my visits meant a lot to him.

Then one Saturday, it must have been a couple of months at least after our first evening together, I was again sitting in his room near the end of another evening. It was a foul night: gusts of rain, driving before a clamorous wind, were sweeping in veils across the Square outside. When it was time for me to go, he looked me full in the face and, as if he had been nerving himself for this moment, he said, 'Why don't you stay here tonight? You can go across to the block in the morning.'

For a few moments our gazes met without anything said. I was wholly sober and whatever decision I made would be completely my own. There would be no difficulty in staying the night. If you booked out at the guardroom you had to check back in by 2359 hours, known loosely to civilians as midnight. But if your plans were more personal, more ambitious and likely to be more satisfying you simply left the camp unofficially at one of the insecure points in the boundary hedge and returned, the following day, by the same route.

However, back to Vic. I knew that his flat contained only the one bedroom and his intentions were tolerably plain, even to me, ingenuous though I was. About the details I was, of course, in utter ignorance: all I knew of the possibilities was what I had gleaned from a thousand barrack-room jokes, scabrous and crude as they always were. For the first time I felt the stirring of a faint curiosity; after all, I could always, when it came to the moment, say no. There was the merest anticipation of what I came later to recognise as lust. It would be pleasant not to cross that bleak barrack-square, head down against the wind and the rain; not to have to endure, later, the clumsy stumblings of the returning revellers, the anonymous and protracted fartings, the occasional puking and the sour-sweet stink of vomit.

'All right,' I said.

About the sleeping arrangements he was quite matter-of-fact. He found spare pyjamas, allowed me to use the tiny bathroom first and settle down in bed. I almost forgot I was on the verge of a unique, perhaps immoral, experience, certainly one that would be generally condemned. Indeed, if detected I should be expelled from the Service and so my life would probably be saved. Ironic. But later, oddly perhaps, I did not feel that anything very heinous had happened.

In the morning he was out and about before I was awake. He brought me a cup of tea to bed. It was luxury, especially to drink it from a proper cup instead of the crude one-pint mugs supplied by the RAF. We had breakfast together; not much was said. Once we caught each other's eye and smiled faintly but for the rest were very matter of fact. The previous night was not mentioned but I realised, and I am sure that he did too, that we had passed a milestone in our relationship: we must now either finish completely with each other or deepen that relationship.

A good half-hour before the Naafi staff came on duty I let myself out of the back entrance, pushed my way into the spinney and through the hedge and stood in the lane at a spot where I could not be seen by anyone inside the camp. On the other side of the lane was a flat potato-field stretching into infinity that misty morning. A few yards further on I re-entered the camp, quite near to the block, and returned to the billet without any further attempt at concealment.

Most of my comrades were still in bed; drinking mugs of the hot sweet tea brought over illicitly from the cookhouse, reading the *News of the World* (whose later slogan was to be ' All human life is there', a sentiment modified by many of its readers by the qualification . . . 'so long as it's between the navel and the kneecaps'). There was some sporadic conversation, mostly about the prowess of various football teams; someone was coughing desperately. The room stank.

' 'Allo, you dirty stop-out,' said Bert, cheerily. 'So you've joined the ranks of the bad boys. I should never have thought it of you.'

From then on Saturday meant our quiet and friendly supper together, though it seemed politic not to spend every Saturday night there, too. I could always sense Vic's eagerness but he never pestered me, never reproached when I got up to go. I soon realised that the relationship was one of deep fulfilment on his part and of a certain quiet and comfortable affection on my own. Lifelong marriages have been founded on less. I did not think ahead: as did all aircrew, I lived only in the moment. The future was at best a philosophical abstraction. The crew-room was constantly sprinkled with new faces: it would have been folly and presumption for any of us to have made plans which presupposed our survival – the Greeks called something very like it 'hubris'. I could ignore all this: I knew that Vic could not, although he never mentioned his fears.

Inevitably the blow fell. One afternoon my own crew went out on a trip and did not return. (Not for us the American word 'mission' or even the official 'operational flight': for us the word 'trip' said all that needed saying). We broke cloud cover over a power-station in north-west Germany only to find that we were awaited and that many fingers were on many triggers. Within seconds our poor kite was a flying bonfire from which all three of us extricated ourselves urgently, our parachutes only just having time to open as our machine crashed heavily into a field where it burned noisily away. We had managed, in the short time available, to jettison the bombs (which exploded with no effect except to scare the hell out of a large herd of cows grazing nearby: within a very short time they had resumed grazing, ignoring the blazing wreck). Minutes later frantic figures, waving an assortment of firearms, and mostly babbling with excitement and incoherent rage, had surrounded us and we were marched away.

Captivity was protracted, boring, often deeply unhappy, an endless and many-faceted deprivation. After the first few months we were allowed to send two air-letters and four postcards every month and incoming mail was unrationed. All my letters, of course, went home; with the cards I tried to keep in touch with many friends. Once, only, I sent a card to Vic, but I did not hear from him and soon I had forgotten him wholly. That stage of my life had been only transient and was now over; my dreams of a post-war world which, presumably I was now destined to see, did not include him.

Five years later, all but a few weeks, I did return home.

The newspapers were full of pictures showing contingents of ex-prisoners: dazed, incredulous, empty faces doing their utmost to look happy for the photographer. Truth was, when you had spent years disciplining yourself against the poison of hope, then hope fulfilled spent itself on that effective armour. When you had used, for years, every device to silence the voice which spoke so compellingly of the need for an interchange of affection – if not with women, then with parents, with children, even with animals, damn it – then that voice stayed silent even now, when acceptable objects of affection were there all around you. Like many others, I was emotionally numb: freedom was too great a gift to comprehend. It would take time to thaw, to adjust to a new, and old, life-style.

Then one day there came a letter from Vic. Chiefly, of course, he wanted us to meet and it would have been churlish to refuse. I had no flicker of intention to resume any kind of relationship: all that, I knew, was a very dead part of earlier days. I had neither wish nor need to revive all that; besides, it hadn't meant so terribly much at the time. But the least I could do was to meet him, once. So I went up to Nottingham and called at the address he had given. It was a small terraced house, neat and tidy inside and out. Vic lived alone and had found a job in a local factory – after my departure, he told me, he felt he wanted to take a more direct part in the war effort so he had got a job in a factory near home, turning out parts for tank engines. It must have been quite a wrench to give up his comfortable billet and his flat with Naafi but I felt it was in some way to do with what he had felt about my own departure from the scene. He looked no different than he had done five years earlier but we met with some difficulty: the old, easy relationship was no longer there. Nothing unusual about that, now: the same strained nothingness was there between me and my, nominal, nearest and dearest. However, he had read all the advice given out for the benefit of the families and friends of returning ex-PsOW, and was obviously trying to let me make the running.

After a rather-strained meal we went out to look at central Nottingham, finishing up later that evening at the Black Boy. The pub was, of course, crammed with the uniforms of all the fighting services of all the allied nations and the wearers were happy. The noise level was high. I didn't enjoy being there and drank very little; before long we left. It seemed to be expected that I would stay the night: on my arrival I had been told to

86

dump my kit in the spare bedroom, so before long I said goodnight and retired.

It was not really a surprise to wake, later, and find I was not alone in the bed. For the first time since my return I was conscious of a faint stirring of emotion, a kind of tenderness – or was it pity? For his part, obviously, he felt as deeply as ever. For him, lovemaking was the deepest emotional fulfilment, an act involving the body and also the mind. On my part it was less: physical easing, of course, but some degree of renewed affection. When we parted, the following morning, we had already agreed another meeting, a fortnight or so later.

Soon I found a job with a large firm not too far from home. I had no thought of moving to Nottingham, and if Vic ever considered moving south, so as to be nearer, I never gave him any encouragement to suggest the matter. It would be enough for me, if not for him, if we met occasionally. He was a satisfying companion: to his earlier love of Shakespeare he had added an attachment to the music of Brahms, almost unknown to me, and this I found all of a piece with the tragedies. His thinking was appreciably different from my own on many things, politics in particular, but the gap was rarely too great and we found a lot of common ground for discussion. We could, with ease on both sides, go for long periods without feeling the need for talk, and this was both restful and unusual, and when Vic managed to buy a small prewar Morris Eight we spent many happy weekends together, and an occasional longer holiday.

My family knew only that I went off for frequent walking tours with a friend who lived in Nottingham; and after I had deflected several suggestions that he should come down to us for a visit it was accepted that we liked to use our time in more salubrious areas: not even my mother would defend Luton on those grounds.

I always knew, of course, that while the relationship was utter fulfilment for him, for me it was only an episode – however agreeable. One night, I remember, we were lying side by side in the dark, afterwards. There had been a long silence but I knew that he was still awake.

'It has to be you,' he said. 'It wouldn't work with anyone else. It wouldn't be the same.'

I murmured something. After a long silence he spoke again.

'One day,' he said, 'one day all this is going to fade out, you know.'

I made some kind of non-committal noise; he was right, I knew: I was gradually moving in a different direction.

'You'll never know how grateful I am,' he said, quietly. He was speaking very deliberately, as if he had thought out and rehearsed all this, and indeed, perhaps he had.

'These last few years – well, nobody could have been happier. Certainly not one of Them. But I do know that for you it's different. I've never tried to kid myself. Well, when the time comes, I'll break clean. You can trust me for that, not to spoil what we've had. I shan't beg or implore or come all that best-years-of-my-life stuff. You can't make things better that way. But I shall always remember. Always. And I shall always feel the same way. Always,' he repeated.

I began to realise, all over again, what he felt. I wondered what kind of a future lay ahead for him – for I knew he was right. For a long time now I had felt a growing need, an increasing curiosity. I wanted to be like my friends: to be part of a two in a two-orientated society, to be wholly accepted, to be able to speak and live freely, not to have to conceal any more. Even so, at that moment I was stirred by a huge and unwonted compassion: I reach out and touched his shoulder briefly. In the darkness he turned his head; I think I heard him sigh; he might even have smiled.

'Thank you for that,' he said quietly.

Soon I was asleep.

For a few months more things went on as usual, then I met Jacky. There had been some kind of function at the local Baptist church which I had got into the habit of attending and at eleven or so that night we all spilled out into Ramillies Drive.

Most people moved purposefully away but a small knot of us lingered on the pavement. There was a full moon; it was a warm night in early June. Opposite me stood a girl whom everyone called Doreen; I had seen her, vaguely seen her, around the church in the preceding weeks or even months, but that evening I was somehow very conscious of her. She was fair and vivacious, and smiled readily; her complexion seemed to owe nothing to cosmetics yet conveyed a peaches-and-cream impression. I realised that I found her most attractive. When the group dispersed it seemed that she and I were going in the same direction. On an uncharacteristic impulse I offered her a lift on the crossbar of my bike and she accepted.

We went slowly up the Drive, speaking very little. Somewhere we passed through a wall of perfume from the night-scented stock in a garden; the wind of our passage blew her long hair most preciously into my face. Her proximity roused strange and strong emotions. As we turned the corner of her road, there in the distance were the lights of a fairground a hundred yards or so past her home; the wind brought snatches of amplified noise. For once I did not hesitate: how different things might have been had I done so.

'What time are you due home?' I asked.

'My parents don't mind,' she replied.

So we parked the bike behind her front hedge and for the next hour we sampled all that the fair could offer. I had never before realised to what extent the various rides are designed to heighten a sense of propinquity, to provide opportunity for the dominant male to guard the helpless female with a supportive arm. All my emotions that night were mint-new, devised then and there for me alone. Long before we left I was utterly besotted – though I did point out, as we strolled slowly home, that Doreen was not my favourite name and that I was going to call her Jacky. To this she made no objection.

We met two nights later – the intervening days were both barren and feverish – and for the first time ever, at the age of twenty-eight, I found myself sitting on one of the double seats in the back row of the Odeon, ignoring the film and conscious only of the girl beside me, her head on my shoulder and my arm possessively around her. For the first time ever I kissed a girl a long reluctant goodnight and went home with my emotions still molten.

Three weeks later my firm sent me up to Staffordshire on a training course which was to last a whole fortnight. The first evening in the hotel into which I had been booked I sat down, of course, to write a long letter to Jacky but to my astonishment and joy there was a letter from her waiting for me on the breakfast table the following morning. She had arranged an early holiday from work and had invited herself to stay with a cousin who lived no more than twelve miles away from where I now was and conveniently on a branch railway line. Her intention was to get as much time with me as I could arrange. The following Thursday my timetable showed as free for research: question sheets would be supplied. I met her at the station that morning, wondering whether the same feelings would still be there when I saw her again – but I need not have worried.

The whole of that day we spent strolling idly over Cannock Chase, stopping frequently to check and express all over again the power of the bond between us. At the end of that long, lovely day I put her into her train and stood on the platform while the engine hissed and hooted its imminent departure. She leaned down; her hair fell over my face. Concealed behind it she said, 'Well, are we engaged, then, now?' I pulled her head down the last few inches to answer her in the only possible way; there was a final hoot and a chuntering and the train started to move. I stood there waving, so wholly submerged in emotion that all thought was dead. Or at least anaesthetised. This, at last, had to be right, hadn't it? This was what all the books and the songs and the films were about; now, at last, I was in the mainstream of life . . .

We saw each other every couple of days and quite a lot of the evenings also; I paid little attention to the course, but fortunately the whole thing was an exercise in empire-building, as so many such courses are, and the meat of the thing could easily be picked up in the revision of the final days. It also helped that there was no terminal examination.

Just before those days scheduled for revision, Jacky had to return home: her nominal week's holiday could be stretched no longer. We sat in the Copper Kettle, where the waitress had long ago sized up the situation and had taken to mooning over us. We discussed practicalities. She would not tell her parents: that would have to wait until I was there and could tell them myself. Equally, of course, she would tell no one else. I guaranteed not to tell my own family.

Two days later, on my final day in Stafford, came a letter from Jacky's father, saying how pleased they were for us. From something he said I gathered that all of Jacky's friends also knew and approved. So much, I thought, for promises but I did not hold it against her: already I was participating in the life-long male game of making extra allowances for females, and doing it with joy. Of course the dear soul was excited; it would have been unreasonable to expect her not to tell her parents. I expect she swore each of her friends to secrecy – which is, of course, almost the equivalent of not telling them at all.

Vic and I had long planned that the last week in July that year we would take the car, for the first time ever, across to the Continent and tour Germany. I would be able to show him my last POW camp and air the shreds of the language which I had picked up during my stay. We would take a tent and camp; we might even get as far down as Bavaria; we had pored long over maps and sketched-out possible routes. Our letters had been full of suggestions and counter-suggestions. I knew that Vic was looking forward intensely to the trip. And now I had the job of telling him, with only three weeks to go, that the whole thing was off. Not only that: our whole relationship was over. Fortunately, neither of us was on the telephone and I could sit down and write a careful letter. There was no need to tell him very much: I knew he had long foreseen this moment; in a vague way, too, I knew how much he would suffer. As the

91

French say: 'There is always one who loves and one who is loved;' there had never been any doubt, in our years together, that for us the saying was true. He wrote back very briefly, almost formally, and bravely, but behind the laconic words I sensed the desolation. I sensed it but I did not feel it: all my feelings were centred on Jacky – there was nothing left over for anyone or anything else.

In August I went off for a week with Jacky and her family in Bournemouth. In pre-Jacky days I would have scorned the idea of wasting a week in such a way: staying in a small hotel and spending our days walking along the front, or window-shopping, or wandering through some famous gardens – whose name escapes me now. Evenings we spent at a concert or a cinema, and for me the programme was of only minor importance. All my values and tastes had changed: being with Jacky was like possessing the Philosopher's Stone: in her presence the dullest, humblest, boringest occupation became suffused with magic, became a means of deep fulfilment. Nothing new about all this, of course: the miracle – or the illusion – works at some time or another for most young men – for a time, at least. I suppose that the effect on myself was the greater for having come, comparatively, so late; the war and five years of captivity had delayed all the usual experiences of life. But now I had caught up and lived in bliss.

Soon after that holiday was over Vic and I met just once more. It was at his request – characteristically, he had added that I need fear no outbursts of temperament; I think that it was just that he needed to know for certain that it was all over – that there could be no crumb of hope left. I went because I felt I owed him at least that. The difficulty was in convincing Jacky that I had to have a weekend away and that she might not come. In the end it had to be a lie: I invented an all-male gathering to set up a Squadron association, and excused myself for the deception by stressing the fact that if indeed it was a lie, then it was a lie told for her peace of mind. But the lie rankled.

Vic and I met in a small hotel near Shrewsbury which we had

often used in the old days. As always, we shared a twin-bedded room and after an evening of unsatisfactory conversation, loose ends trailing and not to be retrieved, we retired. Tonight the three feet or so between our beds was an unbridgeable chasm. We lay in the dark, not speaking, waiting for sleep. I could think only of being again with Jacky, the following evening; the past years had ended, like coming to the final page of a book.

After a long time he asked quietly, 'So it's really all over?'
'Yes'.

Then there was silence again, only after a time I realised that he was weeping quietly, with dignity, because he could not hold back tears. My mind told me that I should feel sorrow for him but I could trigger no emotion whatever. I lay there in the darkness, wholly unmoved, shutting from my consciousness all but the only face that now mattered. The now-stranger wept hopelessly; it was none of my concern and soon I was asleep.

At breakfast we were formal, polite, restrained, and indeed I would not have had it any other way. We parted, later, without even a handshake.

The months passed and both families were soon immersed in preparations for the great day. That is, all the females were immersed: Jacky's father and I exchanged many resigned glances at some latest eruption of female frenzy and I just wished it was all over. So far as I was concerned, we would just have gone quietly to a register office, completed the formalities and come back home to a kind of extra Christmas dinner. But it was not to be. I did broach the idea once but was met by blank incomprehension, soon followed by scorn. For some excellent reason which I have completely forgotten the only possible date was in February. Her parents, it turned out, had recently been left no less than three houses in the neighbourhood and one of these came conveniently vacant, so our home had been chosen for us. Relays of friends turned up and helped us get the place more or less as we wanted it; it was decided that in the new year I should move in alone but until then I should continue to live at home.

November came and with it, almost unheeded in the impending greater occasion, my birthday. I came down to breakfast that morning to find the usual small pile of cards and a few small packages beside my plate. I tried to open them all with one hand while prising loose segments of grapefruit with a spoon held in the other. The segments clung tenaciously and the mail easily avoided being opened unless accorded the customary two hands, so I ate and opened and ate and opened. The first two parcels were from Jacky (gold cufflinks, very swish) and her parents (a gold tie-chain to go with the links). I would have to get used to wearing it, at least for a time. The third packet seemed to be a small, longish box, well wrapped in green paper. I opened the parcel with some difficulty - it had not been intended to come open in a hurry - removed the lid and found myself looking in considerable surprise at a perfect red rose, scarcely out of the bud, neatly packed in damp moss. There was no card; the wrappings gave no clue to the sender; the address had been printed in firm and anonymous block capitals; the postmark, on so small a parcel, was even more illegible than usual. I turned the rose over and over in my fingers as if it would yield some clue. At first I thought that the sender had simply forgotten to enclose a card: every Christmas some unsigned card presented a mystery for our solving. My family, meanwhile, were expressing varying degrees of curiosity in babbled questions which I ignored. Reluctantly and slowly, light dawned. 'There's roses: they're for remembrance.' I felt a momentary pang, faint and distant, a pang which I wholly failed to classify, then I had to deal with my family.

'But who could it *be*?' asked my mother, for the umpteenth time. 'It must be someone who knows you well, to know your birthday.'

I simulated utter mystification: after all, what would they think of a bloke sending another bloke a rose for his birthday with a very real, if invisible, message? To them it would have been not only grotesque but also incredible. They would never understand: the whole situation was incomprehensible, impossible. Devotion could only be a matter of parent and child, or male and female; they never doubted that any other demonstration of feeling must be spurious – not to give it any other, brutal, label.

In the end I only half-denied my mother's theory that I had been a dark horse and that somewhere Out There there was a sorrowing woman still carrying a torch for me. That would have been quite permissible, by their code, even enhancing their concept of my image, but there was total and benevolent agreement that Jacky must never know. They were all willing to take part in so happy a conspiracy. Mother carried the bloom away to put it in water and I went off to work as usual. That evening the rose stood on the sideboard: nobody mentioned it (such tact was rare in our family and was all the more noticeable when occasionally people acted so out of character). After a quick glance, I did not look at it again. Briefly I thought of Vic – it must have been, surely? – and decided that I would not write. Nor, of course, would I invite him to the wedding: kinder not to, I thought.

A week or so later Mother and I were working our way through a list of possible guests ('We *must* invite Auntie Clara: she'd be terribly hurt if we invited Anne and not her'). Having covered all the immediate choices we were considering whom we might have forgotten and Mother said suddenly, 'There's your friend up in the Midlands. Victor, was it? You used to be great friends with him. Aren't you going to ask *him*?'

'Oh, no,' I answered. 'He never goes to weddings. He's a confirmed old bachelor and says weddings are very sad occasions. I'll write and let him know.' (I won't, I thought).

'But if he could only see how happy you and Jacky are, he might change his ideas,' she prattled on. Isn't it funny how all females love weddings? They stand outside churches to watch perfect strangers come out hitched. Prurient anticipation, perhaps? Satisfaction that one more link in the chain has been forged and that their function is being endlessly revalidated?

95

'No, mother,' I said firmly. 'He would not come. Just leave it to me to let him know.'

Just then she thought of other possibilities, more invitations which must be sent out for the sake of family solidarity. Vic's name was never mentioned again.

Once Christmas and New Year were over enthusiasm rose to near-hysteria. It was agreed that the bridesmaids should wear pink. Or was it apple-green? Anyway, the choice seemed to be of the utmost importance. I took no part in this, or any other, business: I simply wanted the whole affair over; it was tolerable, all this doodahing, because it made Jacky happy – but I wanted none of it. All three houses were stacked with parcels; the private rooms at the Luttrell Arms were booked: it was agreed that they would make a good job of the reception. The wedding would be at the Baptist church where we had first met. The honeymoon would be spent in Jersey – for one week only, I was glad to note. I do not remember having been on that decision-making committee, either. At one thing, only, I drew the line: I was not, repeat not, going to wear formal dress. Jacky, thinking of the photographs, tried half-heartedly to point out that I owed a duty to all concerned – even to future generations – but with a determination fuelled by fires of naked panic I was obdurate. She already knew me well enough to distinguish between 'No, but you might be able to talk me into it,' on the one hand, and 'No, bloody bloody No,' on the other and she was in no doubt, after a couple of probing sessions, which degree of negative she had met over this matter.

The Great Day dawned, ran its course, was endured and, mercifully, went. There is no need to go into details; each family constructs the ritual around the same basic pattern. For hour after dreadful hour I repeated mentally the effectual cant-rap: 'This, too, will pass', and waited desperately for the time when I could get down from the stage and stop performing. Finally, of course, we were sitting, just the two of us, in a train; I am sure that I did not look like a bridegroom and I certainly did not feel like one. Epithalamion, indeed: I felt more battered than expectant.

That very first night together was everything I had ever imagined. I knew without a doubt that I had been the first man for her. Afterwards we were lying in the darkness and she said, 'It wasn't the first time for you.' It could equally well have been a question or a statement; I chose to regard it as the second and made no reply. She waited until it was clear that I was not going to speak and then she said very quietly, 'I saved myself for you. It wasn't your first time, was it?'

Thus directly challenged, I replied simply, 'No.' It would have been quite impossible to explain: such things were totally beyond her comprehension and her imagination alike. Yet the bare answer was insufficient: she probed: 'Did you love her?'

While I was considering how little I could say, how I could divert her, she said, 'Of course, they say it's different for men.'

It was a helpful lead. I could reply only, 'Yes, it's different. But whatever it was, it's all over. Very, very over. Now there's only you.'

Then there was quiet; she never mentioned the matter again.

The week was bliss: peace, quiet, comfort, beauty and each other. Even so, when we were finally packing to leave I realised dimly that I would not have wanted a second week: I thought with pleasurable anticipation of various odd jobs waiting for me: of the chance to play some of my records and read some of the books which had been among the presents; of resuming my daily crossword (every day for the past week had started, as it were, with a hiatus); even of going over to the Admin block at work and catching up on recent events. Then there was the Dining Club: another evening was due – one of the customary stag evenings: I anticipated pleasurably some uninhibited male talk. There were two books on reservation at the library, one of them eagerly awaited, having been written by an old friend. Jacky, I now knew, did not read – apart from the women's glossies, of which she seemed to read every one, and some kind of weekly devoted to the doings of the people who acted in films.

'Stars', she called them. She was also devoted to radio soap operas and to a twice-weekly TV serial: her home had one of the earliest sets and in fact I had seen my first programmes there. Before she and I had met, I remembered, I had denounced scathingly and often those same magazines and those same programmes. Well, no doubt she was good for me: I ought to be more tolerant. In my mind was a hazy vista of endless evenings spent reclining comfortably, side by side, blinking placidly at the simulated glowing logs of the gas fire, with the TV set (her father's present) functioning in the corner. Then there would be no lack of more intimate moments: so far as what are called conjugal duties are concerned, there was none of that shut - your - eyes - tight - dear - clench - your - fists - and - think - of - England (men are such beasts); true, her eyes were often shut, but her fists certainly weren't clenched, and if her mother had ever warned her that ladies don't move, there was no sign of it. I remembered briefly how Tommy Wren had described it all to me many years ago: vivid if crude, and smiled. We arrived back to a huge welcome. Jacky and her mother went into a feminine huddle, talking intensely to each other in low voices. I hated to imagine what they might be discussing. Then soon we were permitted to go home together and make a start on our new life.

Over the following months all my anticipations were realised yet somehow the reality was ever so slightly less ecstatic than the fantasy had been. It was a pleasing novelty to find every wish foreseen almost before I had formulated it even mentally; after the slap-happy days of bachelordom it was a joy to find my shirts not only ironed and neatly folded, but with every button in place. When I arrived home of an evening my slippers would appear, closely followed by a drink and, after just the right interval, a meal. My remarks about the incidents of the day would be not only heard but keenly anticipated: the ongoing serial of my daily life needed no 'the-story-so-far' to introduce the latest instalment. At the weekends there was the garden to be got into order, though I was and am no gardener;

fortunately, Jacky's father was and came over often.

For the first few months we went over to Jacky's old home for Sunday dinner, but one day Jacky announced that she was now confident that she would not let the side down and from then on we alternated most Sundays, sometimes going to my own mother. And always we were together, as I had so keenly anticipated, yet somehow, somehow, the reality was just short of total bliss. My wife, as I had now got used to calling her (and how strange it had sounded at first) was less than enthusiastic about my occasional evenings out, at the stag evenings of the club or the annual squadron re-union. After all, I pointed out, she had all day every day to be with her mother and her women friends, to chat over peculiarly-feminine matters or to go drifting aimlessly but happily around the shopping centre. She gossipped endlessly about someone called Edie whom, some-how, I never met. I wouldn't even mind her spending the occasional evening in such activities: I could always catch up on some reading or listen to some music (Jacky was not very fond of my kind of music, preferring the catchy tune of the moment. I never dared tell her what I thought of the kind of noises she preferred to listen to.) She didn't think much of my attempts to excuse my occasional private outings: once I got home from work, plainly, it was ungrateful and unnatural of me to want to do anything without her. Well, whatever her views, there were some sacrifices I was not prepared to make.

Every Saturday morning we would go out together; my first call was always at the library after which I would meet her at one of the shops on the list which she always gave me for this purpose. Somehow, I began to feel vaguely, somehow . . . But it would have been treachery to have followed the thought to its logical conclusion and my mind always responded to the reins and turned aside. In the office one day I remarked to Sanders, 'You know, there can't really be such a place as heaven. Continuing happiness is pretty pointless. You could almost call it boring.'

He looked at me across the canteen table, smiled slightly (he had been married for some fifteen years) and replied, 'Oh, so you've found that out, have you? Marriage has changed you.'

'I don't see the connection,' I answered, puzzled, but he declined to follow the topic any further.

One day, however, I picked up my well-thumbed copy of Three Men on the Bummel and found my own sentiments expressed exactly in the opening pages. In cold print the words could be re-read, examined in detail and mulled over; behind the comedy there was, I realised, truth. Still, I was deeply contented – well, most of the time. As much as was good for me, perhaps, I told myself: what else was there to want?

Like most women, I find, Jacky planned ahead: birthdays, Christmas, family celebrations of any kind. Always there was something to look forward to or, as the case sometimes was, not. That next November both families came to us on my birthday: Jacky had cooked and baked and washed and cleaned for the occasion. As I let my mother into the house it was plain to me that she had something on her mind. She checked conspiratorially that we were alone in the hall and could not be overheard.

'It's come again,' she whispered.

'What's come again?'

'Remember last year? The rose? Well, another box came this morning. I've got it here in my bag. I bet it's a rose again.'

'Well, take it back home,' I said firmly. 'If Jacky sees it, she'll want to know all about it. And anyway (remembering) I don't know who sent it, do I?'

'All right, dear,' said my mother. 'But you really ought to get in touch with her and get it stopped.'

'I can't,' I said forcefully. 'I don't know where it came from.'

Mother, I could see, was touched at the thought of so faithful a lover: within her frame of reference such fidelity was to be both pitied and admired. If she had known, if she could have grappled with the reality, what would her feelings then have been? Shock, horror, disgust, incredulity, total incomprehension? I wished indeed that Vic would stop (if indeed it really was Vic, and yet who else could it have been?). Still, I was determined

100

not to write: even one short and necessary letter might have been interpreted as the end of a fragile cord which might, perhaps, lead to the bridging of a gap. If I said nothing, Vic would have to stop. He must see that the old days were dead and buried, that nothing was to be gained by any kind of relationship, even the most tenuous. You couldn't go on feeling that way about someone indefinitely, surely?

Over the next few years I came to see, slowly and reluctantly, that Jacky and I were not exactly the soul-mates which I had once assumed we were – or could become. In the early years of our marriage, years of necessary adjustment, I knew, I tried to get her to go out to an occasional concert or theatre; neither of these were to her taste and after a few unsatisfying experiments she declined any further invitations. That meant, of course, that I could not go, either. She, for her part, tried to get me to go to the occasional dance or even, horror, to one of the discos which were then just starting. Impelled by curiosity I did poke my head one evening into the back room of the Luttrell Arms, and was horrified to find near-darkness lit only by revolving coloured lights. There was an unbearably-amplified ugly noise rising and falling, a raucous voice mouthing distorted vowels, expressing (in the few minutes I stayed) the most banal and repetitious ideas: adolescent wailings of frustrated lust, wrongly identified as love. I glimpsed vaguely idiotic forms jerking spasmodically in all directions from the loins. This was, most definitely, not for me. I tried to explain this to Jacky without any direct or implied criticism of the kind of taste which would seek out such a place and remain there more than a few minutes but it was clear that she was offended and for the rest of that evening we were cooler to each other than we had ever before been. So we tended to spend most evenings at home. Occasionally we went over to one of the in-laws and occasionally some of our relatives came over to us. But there were many long evenings when we were on our own. She would watch the TV, uncritically accepting whatever it served up, leafing through her magazines, offering me spasmodically the trivia of her day:

gossip and speculation about friends, neighbours and relatives; titbits of scandal gleaned from the daily tabloid or from her film magazine; scraps of information which had stuck on their haphazard way through her mind, straining the impressions of the day. I would struggle over the few remaining bits of my crossword (rarely could I finish it without that prolonged wrestling of an evening) and then fall back on the current book. Occasionally we would wrangle mildly over the choice of a TV programme: there was an occasional offering which I wanted to see. There were two channels at the time and then soon there was a third. I liked documentaries of all kinds and newsy programmes; Jacky preferred – in fact had an insatiable appetite for – the very worst kind of American trash: fables full of worthless characters punching, swindling, shooting and seducing each other. Soon we were able to afford a small portable set and this I installed in the bedroom; occasionally, therefore, we could be watching different programmes in different rooms. Yet our partnership was still warm and loving and I could not really have asked for more in a wife. We had, I considered, evolved a lifestyle acceptable to us both and when, eventually, we had children the marriage would be doubly complete.

One evening we had both been watching the box, I remember. The usual pre-copulatory drama of a male and a female, this time set against the background of the Napoleonic wars. While we were sitting there an earlier evening came to mind. Vic and I had watched an American version of War and Peace; I had felt him stirring in his seat once or twice and on the way home afterwards he had burst like a bomb. 'Those people out there,' he said bitterly (he meant the whole heterosexual world) 'are obsessed with bloody copulation. Their kind, of course. At the start they show you the bloke and the woman, and you know that after two hours of obstacles dreamed up by the scriptwriters he will be about to poke her. Anything will do for a backcloth: the Russian revolution, the Great War, an expedition down the Amazon or to the north pole or to bloody Mars. It's all just incidental to when he will and how they will finally get around to it. Unless he's a priest, of course, or she's a nun, then you are supposed to enjoy their sadness. All the women weep into piddling little hankies. Sometimes the woman pretends to be a professor of some kind and to prove it she wears specs and one day he gently takes them off and says in some surprise, 'Why, you're beautiful'. Of course she bloody is: she's Gina bloody Lollobrigida and if she wasn't highly shaggable she wouldn't be in the sodding film. And the idiots queue up for hours on winter evenings and go in for the same old dose of bloody dope. And when they do go into the last clinch and the music plays and the credit titles start to roll, you are expected to believe that this really is The End and that from now on they will live Happily Ever After.'

Vic's voice easily suggested the capitals. I listened, fascinated.

'If they only thought about the marriages they were going back home to or the ones they read about in the Sunday papers or the ones they know about, they'd know it wasn't The bloody End at all: just the start of something which will probably go wrong.'

Even allowing for his jaundiced viewpoint and the propaganda, he was largely right, I supposed. I suddenly felt, for the first time in years, the ease of the relationship we had once had; perhaps it was because, being male, we both thought more or less in the same way. Or the fact that we didn't live together, day after day, in the same small house, trying not to get on each other's nerves. From here my thinking took me into forbidden territory. The physical side was not all that different: it largely came from how you felt about your partner, but then the other way there was the double satisfaction of the alternative role. Enough: time I brought my thoughts into order. At least, Jacky and I had had no quarrels; neither of us indulged in displays of temperament. I felt very secure in our marriage.

Later we had our usual evening drink, discussed the night's television and prepared for bed. As usual I went up first while Jacky cleared away the few supper things: she was very tidy and never left the debris of a meal to wait until the morning. I was

103

sitting-up in bed reading when she entered the room and sat down in front of the dressing-table. I registered vaguely that she was doing something feminine with several bottles and jars. After a time and without turning her head, she spoke.

'I've got something to tell you.' I looked up, finger marking the place, and said, 'Oh? Go on, then.'

'I've been going to tell you for a long time but somehow I couldn't find the courage. I'm going away tomorrow. With Jack Longstaff.'

Expecting some fascinating but trivial feminine secret, I had been holding the book at half-cock, waiting for the opportunity to resume my reading. My mind, similarly, was only half engaged. Now the book slid from my hand on to the down-turned sheet, slid over the curve of my thigh and fell to the carpet. I made no attempt to stop it. My mind was in shock, reprocessing what she had just said, checking that she really had said what she seemed to say.

After a time my confused senses could offer only, 'Jack Longstaff? Who's that?'

Wearily she answered, 'It's just like you not to know, isn't it? You don't even bother to know who my friends are. Edie's husband, of course. He's been on the night shift for the last six months so we've been able to spend a lot of time together.' Pause. 'It all started when Edie went in to hospital – remember? I used to go over there to do all the odd jobs.' With an unexpected and uncharacteristic grim humour she remarked, almost aside, 'There was one odd job that neither of us had intended. Anyway we've decided that we can't go on as we are and tomorrow we're leaving. He's got a new job. In London. Tonight he's telling Edie.'

Shocked though I was at what she was telling me, yet I had a brief image of Edie's probable reaction to the news: hysteria, reproaches, pleas, endless, endless tears. Fortunately the nurses were there to look after her; they would probably give her a sedative.

I pulled myself together. 'But . . . ' I said, and stopped.

'It's no use,' she said quietly. All this time, I realised, she had been watching me in the mirror. 'It's final. I'm not right for you. Or you for me. Anyway, I've made up my mind. All my stuff is packed in suitcases in the spare room. I'm leaving after breakfast. I won't worry you about money or anything like that: Jack has enough – more than you'll ever have. It'll be a clean break. You'll be able to divorce me and start again with somebody else. There are plenty of women who would like a safe, boring husband. Good job we never had any kids. Perhaps if we had it might have been different.'

I was still staring dumbly at her face in the mirror, wholly dazed, unable to formulate a clear thought. Then I was going to cry but I made an effort, cleared my throat and tried to decide what to say. There didn't seem to anything *to* say. She rose from the stool, went round to her side of the bed and got in. At no stage did our bodies touch.

She asked, 'Do you want to go on reading?' Her nonchalance was complete. I could not answer but as I did not reach for my book she answered her own question and put out the light. In the darkness, lying with her back to me, as a kind of after-thought she added, 'Even my name wasn't good enough for you, was it? Nobody else ever objected to Doreen. My parents chose it and I never thought there was anything wrong with it. You had to be different. I suppose I ought to have known, then, but I was too young. And, of course, I thought you were marvellous – in those days. Hero back from the war and all that.'

Then there was a long silence. After a time I reached out in the darkness – I do not know why: seeking comfort, perhaps – and touched her shoulder.

'That's no use,' she said wearily. 'That won't work any more. I'm sorry but that's the way it is.'

I withdrew my hand: Even now I had some remnant of self-respect – or was it pride? At any rate I wouldn't grovel. I lay, staring at the invisible ceiling. She had chosen heavy, lined curtains that shut out every chink of light: otherwise, she had said, she found it difficult to sleep. Odd, what trivia floated up from the forgotten depths at a moment of high tragedy. I felt grief rising irresistibly within me; tears welled up in a flood and I heard someone weeping. I tried to weep quietly, perhaps even with dignity. But it was no use: I really was losing her. I really should be completely alone. I should never again try to fashion such a bond: I should hug my misery and remain apart. Curiously, at this moment I knew that I was two people: one self had lost control and was weeping while the other listened dispassionately and was already reaching out towards the future. Into that second intruded a thought: once before I had lain in a darkened bedroom, listening to someone weeping hopelessly, but then it was another. Now, at last, I understood what he had felt.

Eventually, somehow, I slept. When I awoke Jacky was not there but I could hear her moving about below, just as if this was only another morning. From below came the sounds of cups and saucers and the smell of toast and of bacon. But this was not just any day, was it? I got out of bed, went along the landing and opened the door of the spare room. There were three large suitcases and a number of plastic bags. Incongruously I thought of an old joke between us: 'I haven't got a thing to wear.' I half-smiled: already and through the grief which sat like a lump in my stomach, already the healing processes were starting.

I washed and shaved with care, dressed and went downstairs. Breakfast was ready as usual; we exchanged the usual small-talk over the table but today it was brittle, chosen so that each sentence died with its utterance – there could be no follow-up. Today there were fences we might not cross. Today I looked long at the headlines of my paper but when I had read them twice I could still not have told you what they said. Once, only, she faltered in her resolve – I think. She looked at me across the table, opened her mouth to say something, hesitated, said – more to herself than to me: 'No' – and turned back to her plate. I waited but that was all.

I determined to die, if die I must, with dignity and self-control. Our parting was formal, using the minimum of words, our glances never meeting. She promised to send me an address and then a taxi drew up outside. The horn blew. She opened the front door and the driver entered; he went upstairs with her and two loads brought down all her possessions: not much, I thought now, for all our years together. Then the driver stood on the step, waiting for her; in his inhibiting presence I kept a very tight grip on myself. Then she was walking down the path for the last time. The gate failed to latch and slowly swung open again: for weeks I had been meaning to fix that catch and I would definitely do it today. She climbed into the car without a single backward glance and was gone. Characteristically, before leaving she had cleared the table, washed all the breakfast things and put everything away. The place was as tidy as it always was between meals – but now it was uniquely empty, too. Now I was alone, alone in a sense that I had never before experienced. The sunshine streamed through the window, throwing a rectangle of bright light on the grey carpet. Then I realised that I was lying on that carpet – I had no idea how I had got there – my face to the leg of the table. I was weeping uncontrollably, and now with no effort at dignity. After a time I turned my head sideways: next door's cat was sitting on the outside window sill, waiting for the bacon rinds which Jacky always gave him at this time. He regarded me quite incuriously and blinked.

I rose from the floor and willed myself to start again from that moment, recreating my life with what was left to me, trying to expand the other constituents to fill that gap.

The difficult part was having to explain to so many other people, to endure their sympathy, but after a time I ceased to feel much: explanations became automatic, a kind of recorded message. The loss, though, was rather like having a limb amputated: you learn to compensate but things can never again be quite the same. This, I now knew, was how Vic must have felt all those years ago. This year, I resolved, when the rose arrived,

107

I should write back and apologise for the grief which I had caused him.

That year, however, no rose came. I wrote anyway.

A few evenings later the telephone rang and a woman's voice introduced herself as the new owner of Vic's house. Quickly I reviewed mentally what I had written but the discretion of those earlier years had remained: Only Vic would have understood fully the meaning of my words. Vic had sold up some six months previously and gone 'abroad', promising to send back a forwarding address. He didn't. So she had opened my letter in order to return it to me but had decided to ring instead.

'And do you know,' she went on, 'he left the whole place spotless. But when I first went to view the house I was very struck by a beautiful rose-bush in the garden, just under the kitchen window. Beautiful, it was. And the day I moved in, I found it was gone. At first I thought he had dug it up to give it to a friend but when I went outside I found that he had just chopped it down. Just chopped it down. I found it dumped on the compost heap.'

7

Parallel Universe

1 Adolf-Hitler-Stadt
Wesselstrasse 339,
Germany
Home: 010 49 30 4837
University: 010 49 30 6908

11.4.2008

My dear David,

You cannot know how glad I was to hear from you this week; as your godfather I have long felt guiltily aware that I ought to see you more often and, if possible, to be of some help. But then London is a long way off, away from the centre of things.

Before we begin, my warm regards to your parents. We last met, I think, at the Party Congress, in 1998 and I am hoping that you will all be able to come over and spend a couple of weeks here with me. Berlin, as it used to be called, is a very beautiful city; our American and Asiatic visitors always find it impressive.

Now to business. I am glad to see that you still read and write. Since the advent of the talking computer (back in 1975?) these skills have decayed rapidly; after all, the average man does not need them any more, either for work or for pleasure, so why should he bother? Only scholars like myself, tied to our libraries of ancient volumes, still maintain the old skills. And even *our* numbers are dwindling. Are you interested in some kind of

scholastic career? If so, I can help: I have some useful connections, Party as well as state.

Now, in response to your request I have prepared a short
résumé of the period in question; my sources have been largely
German, of course, aided by some files we have here of the
American newspapers of the time. Of course, we now take
European unity as so self-evidently sensible that it is hard to
remember that for most of the second millennium AD Europe
was constantly racked by wasteful and destructive civil wars,
the groupings changing frequently. At least, from 1940 onwards
Europe began to come together under German leadership. The
process was not easy, of course, as I shall describe.

I have drawn heavily on two books which I commend to you:
Europas Schicksalsjahre, by Kurt Deggendorf (Tübingen 1957)
Vorwärts mit der Partei! by Heinz Aschmann (Brockhaus,
1984). Their contents have, of course, been transferred to
audiotape but I do hope that you will read them for yourself.
They are, I suppose, mildly biased towards the German point of
view in those far-off days. I cannot really believe that Adolf
Hitler was wholly the political and military genius that the
books (especially the second one) portray; equally, had the
English records of that time not been so thoroughly destroyed,
we might not have so extreme a view of the English leader,
Winston Churchill. It is unlikely that any national leader of a
nation such as the English then were could be so wholly an
epitome of foolishness

A word of warning – perhaps unnecessary – before you
begin your study. Every historian knows that he must keep
separate in his mind the immediate and the historical aspects of
any great event. The sufferings of a given moment are always
the inevitable and necessary birth-pangs of the future – in this
case, manifestly, a golden future for the European nations of the
late twentieth century. For example, the Roman invasion of
Britain in 55 BC must have appeared to our ancestors (yours
and mine) as an unrelieved disaster; but it was those centuries
of Roman rule that helped bring the country under the rule

110

of a common law. Equally, to a Cheruscan warrior the victory of Arminius over the Romans at the Battle of the Teutoberger Wald in 9 AD must have seemed a great triumph. Yet the Romans withdrew permanently, leaving the Teutonic states to war against each other until they found unity under Bismark as late as 1883. The tardy and new found German nationalism led directly to the two wars, that of 1914 to 1918, and that of 1939 to 1940. Truly, the Chinese say 'Sorrow is the mother of joy.' Since 1940 Europe has come together and now stretches, of course, from the Atlantic to the Urals and from the Arctic Circle to the Mediterranean. From our viewpoint, so long after those fateful days, we can see that any other outcome to that second war would have set back the cause of European unity for more centuries to come.

It is true that in the immediate aftermath there were several years of the most abominable suffering; even now we do not know how bad things were – most of the material of the time was marked 'Secret' and eventually destroyed. There are references in the American newspapers of the period 1940 – 1955 or so, but even these are necessarily incomplete – the European authorities of the time saw to that. That early Nazi heresy of anti-Semitism was responsible for mass murder of the Jews in all European countries: even today, Nazis and Germans are deeply ashamed of the atrocities then committed. Of course, virulent anti-Semitism had been endemic in Europe for many centuries: in earlier ages it raged in Britain, too. Have you ever seen Clifford's Tower, in York? The word 'pogrom' is Russian and after the conquest of Poland many Poles denounced Jewish fellow-Poles to the Germans, knowing well their eventual fate. Since the defeat and breakup of the USSR all the remaining Jews were resettled east of the Fortified Wall, in the area around the Aral Sea. The operation was only a partial success: urbanised Jews found it hard, even impossible, to adjust to life in those harsh surroundings and at so low a standard of living. They died off in the hundreds of thousands. A fortunate few wandered south and managed to reach the land of their remote ancestors and even, later, Greater America. I understand (news is even now hard to come by) that there is still an autonomous and reasonably-stable Jewish state in the area, its people living mainly from farming. More of that later, in its place.

Our present prosperity, together with our internal and external peace, is due to the essential flexibility of National-Socialist thought and (especially) practice. Nazism was never, of course, a coherent political philosophy: it was and is an endless series of pragmatic decisions made minute-by-minute by the Führer or someone deputed by him, in accordance with certain general principles. So today we have a kind of disciplined democracy, still one-party of course, which is vastly different from the Nazism of the early days. Unlike the Marxist state, Nazi apparatus has largely withered away, changed its forms, leaving us with a coherent, peaceful and prosperous society. Our citizens enjoy as high a standard of personal freedom as is compatible with the welfare of the community as an entity. 'Gemeinnutz vor Eigennutz,' as the saying has it: what serves the nation takes precedence over what profits only the individual. How could any sane person of goodwill fail to agree with that? Without the community none of us could live. Communism, that bogey of its day, had the tenacity which is characteristic of all noxious weeds. Once the Europeans under their German Führer smashed the Soviet Union in 1943 and dismembered it, nobody has ever tried to resurrect the spectre of Communism.

Enough, then, by way of introduction. Please read my summary as carefully as you can; remember, it *is* only a summary. Should this give rise to any queries, do ring me at my department, where I have installed a videophone. It would be good to see you again. I wonder how much you have changed; it is almost ten years since we met. I, you will find, am older, fatter and greyer.

Heil Hitler!

Your affectionate godfather,

Tom Jeffries.

The Struggle for European Unity
A short outline from 1940

In the summer of 1940 the British once again faced the probability of an imminent invasion – but that 'once again' needs qualification. There had been two successful invasions of Britain: the Roman landing in 55 BC and the Norman landing in 1066 – a millennium apart. By 1940 that second invasion was also a thousand years back in history and it was with a mixture of confidence and apprehension that the British awaited the latest onslaught. 'Confidence', because the German leader, Adolf Hitler, could surely not succeed where even the great Napoleon had failed? 'Apprehension' because the Germans had already, in a few short months, captured all the countries of western Europe: Norway, Denmark, Holland, Belgium and France. The one remaining country, Spain, was ruled by a government with good reason to be grateful to Germany. In the month or so that it had taken the Germans to overrun France, the British forces there had been expelled; true, no less than 300,000 men had been brought safely back across the moat and into the fortress, but all their equipment had necessarily been abandoned. Artillery, small-arms, tanks and armoured cars, even rifles, all had been lost. In the fighting and the retreat the Royal Air Force had lost almost all of its bombers and most of its fighters based on the European mainland. The Royal Navy had come off comparatively best, having lost mainly small craft.

All in all, the British armed forces were seriously, even dangerously, underequipped to meet an invasion by so well-armed, well-trained, highly-confident and implacable an enemy as the Germans.

What preparations could be made were made. Minefields were laid in the approach waters to the south and east coasts and along the beaches; arrangements were made to set the very sea on fire by pumping out aviation fuel and igniting it; fields behind the coast-line were littered with stakes, tractors, combine harvesters and the like, to deter glider-borne landings. A massive civilian army, extremely poorly armed and of

113

doubtful value, was formed of old soldiers and teenage boys. Speeches were made: 'We will fight them on the beaches,' etc; the Press fulminated vaingloriously and, as usual, ignorantly; women's organisations stood ready to offer tea or bandages, as appropriate. All in all, every conceivable preparation was made. But informed minds harboured grave doubts about the final effectiveness of these warlike posturings. The slogan of the time, repeated from mouth to mouth, was 'You can always take one with you', but thoughtful people knew that even that was not true.

So, as reported above, opinion was divided – but everyone (or almost everyone) concerned was determined to put up a fight when and if the invasion came.

Perhaps the mood of the time was epitomised by an eye-witness account we have of the men of a Royal Air Force station being detailed to their battle-quarters. Each party of men formed up and was in its turn exhorted by a senior officer not to come back alive: they were to die fighting in what he admitted was inevitable defeat. All in all, it was a very un-British occasion.

It it known that the Germans agonised over whether to invade or whether to let the islanders come to terms with their hopeless situation. The first course would mean inevitable heavy losses in the bitter fighting: Britain would not go down as easily as had all the other countries. Yet a Britain defiant could hope for material support from the USA (as it then was) and from its dominions. Moreover, pact or no pact, there was a considerable chance that at some strategic moment the Soviet Union would attack from the east. Germany had always seen a two-front war as the greatest threat; in an effort to avert this possibility it had in 1939 signed a non-aggression pact with the Russians and this also assured them of certain necessary raw materials, albeit at the cost of half of Poland.

So now possibility was weighed against possibility until finally, having listened to all his military leaders, the Führer issued Operation Seelöwe: orders for the third and last invasion of the British Isles.

In late July, before Britain had had a chance to do much more than make the most elementary preparations, the Luftwaffe began a series of systematic raids against Royal Air Force bases and radar stations south and east of a line Norwich-Reading-Portsmouth. The Royal Air Force fought resolutely, despite being heavily outnumbered, and both sides sustained heavy losses; in a war of attrition, however, the Germans were able to accept such a depletion of their forces, whereas the Royal Air Force was not. As soon as mid-August the British bases were mostly out of action and its fighters, now operating from stations north of the Thames, were little able to ward off the endless attacks. It was then that large German forces landed by parachute and gliders at points along the south coast from Bognor to Pevensey. The Royal Navy initially tried to shell these concentrations from the sea but massive attacks from waves of dive-bombers soon caused them losses so heavy that the price was too high: the Navy was forced to withdraw. Under the command of General Kurt Student the invaders fought with great determination. Despite heavy losses, and for a time it almost seemed uncertain whether they would manage to build up their momentum, in the end numbers told (they were reinforced by units brought over, under strong air cover, in whatever shipping could be scraped up from ports in occupied countries as far north as Narvik in northern Norway, and as far south as Bordeaux). The British lacked artillery and armour – some of which, abandoned in France, was now brought over and used against them. All their bravery and ferocity could not make up for that essential weakness. Gradually the beachhead was extended and the defenders fell back, contesting every yard of the way. As they went they destroyed whatever might be of use to the invaders: railway and road bridges, power stations, canals. Many roads were clogged by columns of refugees streaming desperately north and west, and inevitably these suffered heavy losses from air attacks and from artillery.

Within three weeks of the first landings the Germans stood on a line which followed the south bank of the Thames estuary, ran through the suburbs south of London and then curved south and west to Southampton (which was captured almost undamaged in a daring attack by paratroopers).

For a time there was stability: both sides needed respite from the bitter fighting. The British used the pause to take stock of their position: did they really want and intend to lay waste their whole island as they retreated steadily northwards – as now seemed inevitable? In any case, how much longer could they continue to fight? American supplies, necessarily carried only in British shipping (according to an act of Congress) were weakened by constant submarine attacks. Did it make sense to destroy the infrastructure and to litter the land with millions of corpses so that a cadre could retreat overseas to continue the fight, as best possible, from bases thousands of miles away?

The answer to all these questions pointed in one direction only. On October 13th, a Friday, the recently-appointed commander of all British forces asked for an armistice to discuss terms for a possible settlement. These terms, it turned out, were comparatively liberal. All foreign citizens, ie, military personnel of the Commonwealth and empire, might be repatriated under German supervision; all weapons of war, including ships and aircraft, were to be handed over to the Germans; all military personnel were to return to their bases and there await, under German guard, their eventual disposition; all German PsOW were to be handed over at once. In addition, British colonies everywhere were to come under direct German supervision. There were some financial provisions to do with reparations. As an afterthought, all males not in the armed forces but between the ages of 18 and 39 were to hold themselves in readiness for compulsory non-military service, for an unspecified period, anywhere in the world. Clearly, Germany was thinking to her new-found colonies.

Politically, the Royal Family might stay or leave the country to any destination of their choice: they soon, in the event, left for Australia. Parliament was suspended and all political parties were declared dissolved. Britain was to come under the control of a military governor, General von Falkenhausen; he, it turned out, spoke fluent English, was to prove himself scrupulously fair and was even, perhaps, an admirer of things British. Above all, he was a soldier and not a Party man.

Most of the British War Cabinet had, as soon as the armistice was requested, left the country for an unannounced destination, accompanied by many national figures who had reason to fear for their safety in a Britain controlled by a Nazi Germany. Once the terms had been accepted, and really there was no choice, the British nation was represented vis-à-vis the Germans by a small emergency cabinet composed of men from the armed forces, the Civil Service, business and commerce, together with a few minor politicians who considered that their new overlords would consider them to be no danger in the new set-up. It was, of course, known that the German secret police, the Gestapo, had a list of many people they intended to arrest; many of these people had seized the opportunity to escape the country with what was now to be the government-in-exile; others went to ground, assuming minor identities in remote parts of the country; many simply went to Eire, assuming that the Germans would respect Irish neutrality. Now the fighting stopped; the troops dispersed to their regimental depots, which had become, in effect, prison camps guarded by units of the Wehrmacht; refugees started the trek back to their homes – or to what was left of them. There was a general feeling of relief mingled with foreboding.

Technically, the various Dominions were still at war with Germany but as they were all thousands of miles away – indeed, Australia and New Zealand were on the other side of the world – it was quite impossible for them to carry on any meaningful kind of war; in any case, it would have been quite senseless as things now were. Within the next month or so all of them signed armistices and agreed to negotiate a full peace settlement at a later date.

So, as the winter of 1940 set in, Germany was the undisputed and total master of Europe. The other two giants, east and west,

117

the USA and Japan, pondered the new situation; in the Kremlin there was much heartsearching: to what extent could they now rely on their treaty-partner, now in an impregnable position and with all her former enemies defeated? Japan had taken over vast British, French and Dutch possessions around the Pacific, announcing the formation of the Greater East Asia Co-Prosperity Sphere – under Japanese hegemony. The Italians had spread along the whole southern Mediterranean coast and had added erstwhile British Somalia, with German approval, to its new Ethiopian colony; the United States, alarmed (and with cause) had called a conference of all the governments of all the states of the Americas. The world was dividing into huge blocks, each a super-power in its own right.

In May of 1941 the Germans held a victory parade in London; Hitler took the salute before the Cenotaph in Whitehall. Among the forces participating in the march-past was the first contingent of the newly-formed Legion of Saint George: British volunteers who took their place within the SS, together with similar units from each of the other defeated nations. The Germans trumpeted the occasion as a demonstration of European unity; those British in the crowd – relatively few – looked on in sad or sullen silence. With this occasion, an unhappy one for the British, the last European war – and probably the last war ever to be fought among the world's major powers – was over. Or almost, as will be seen: there remained one piece of unfinished business.

As soon as the German terms had been accepted and the Treaty of Berlin signed in late 1941, the process of Gleichschaltung had begun in conquered Britain. This word was much in use by the Nazi party of the time; it has since, of course, fallen into disuse – there has been no need for it in the last half-century or more. Quite simply it means neutralisation or paralysis of any organisation, of any kind, which might offer resistance to Nazi ideas and practice. Beyond this again, it denoted the further process of connecting up a nation's life-system, as it were, to Nazi sources. So Britain and especially London filled up with German officials and

118

functionaries, most of them uniformed. At first the British maintained a barrier of cold hostility to the newcomers, working with them in a machine-like way and refusing all social contacts. But it had to be admitted that these alien people in their smart uniforms were behaving absolutely correctly and slowly the barriers crumbled: young men and young women eyed each other across the gap of nationality, and ideology proved weaker than sexual attraction, as it had done throughout history.

The last months of 1940 and the beginning of the following year had seen a great deal of change. Doctor Josef Goebbels, the Minister for Propaganda and Popular Enlightenment, set up an office which thenceforth effectively controlled all the media: newspapers, radio, (there was at the time of course no TV) films, magazines. In addition, a new bureau was to report on all books currently in print or in the public libraries and recommend which should be withdrawn and destroyed; in future, publishers of all kinds would have to submit all scripts and obtain authorisation for publications. Reichsführer SS Heinrich Himmler spent some weeks in London; from its new HQ in Scotland Yard the Reichssicherheitshauptamt (RSHA) started operations to control many aspects not only of the nation's life but of the lives of all kinds of private individuals. People learned not to look too ostentatiously out of the window when a large black car stopped outside the house of a neighbour and men in long overcoats were seen to escort away someone still, obviously, in night attire. Nor did they comment when it was announced that the person arrested had died of a heart attack while in 'protective custody.' If they sympathised with the family, even that they did in terms which could not be construed as hidden resentment.

As in Germany, people soon learned to recognise agents of the Gestapo, to look to one side and to increase their pace until they were well away, relieved that at least the knock had not come to their own door. It was a time when friend learned not to speak too freely to the friend of many years; when husband and wife guarded their tongues before their own children; when it was safe to move briskly from one end of a street to another, looking neither to left or right – but not to show awareness of what could hardly be overlooked. There was a smell of fear in the very air.

The names Heydrich and Kaltenbrunner awoke fear, yet none could say when or under what circumstances they had heard them.

Reichsmarshal Hermann Goering created himself a Marshal of the Royal Air Force, in place perhaps of the departed King George, and was seen in public in uniform – though with considerably more gold braid than previous holders of the rank had permitted themselves. This rather endeared him to his new subjects: at least it showed that 'Fatty' was human; although he was part of the Nazi apparat, he awoke more gentle amusement than fear.

It was a time when Britain was being connected in every way with the veins and arteries of the Reich; the country soon functioned organisationally as did the other occupied territories – even Germany itself.

Some manifestations made daily life difficult even for the circumspect. The Reichsmark had been pegged at a rate of exchange so monstrously advantageous to the invaders (8 to the pound sterling) that soon the shops were bare of clothing, jewellery, pictures and other desirable items. The occupation troops, officials and functionaries at all levels, were responsible for a flood of parcels which overloaded the postal services back to Germany. Food rationing was tightened and some foods not as yet rationed became available only against coupons: bread, vegetables, fish. Even restaurant meals entailed having coupons clipped – as had long been the case in Germany itself.

More sinisterly for the British, large camps were constructed in remote parts: the Scottish Highlands, the Yorkshire Moors, mid-Wales, among others. Around these camps there were exclusion zones policed by armed troops who had instructions to fire on anyone not submitting to arrest. The existence of these camps might not be mentioned in the media, but even so the secret could not be kept. Many prominent people vanished and, it was rumoured, were being 're-educated' in these camps. Some people were shipped directly to Germany: despite all the warnings about dangerous talk, yet the railwaymen and the ferry crews could not or would not keep wholly silent. Those Jews who had not managed to escape the country – very difficult to do as the only possible haven was Ireland and all means of travel were, of course, tightly controlled, either went 'underground' or simply waited fatalistically until one day they were arrested and seen no more. There were reports, told in hushed voices, of long trains of closed goods waggons heading for Channel ports.

Life had changed unimaginably and in so short a time. An air of fear and oppression brooded over the land, nor was there any possible deliverance to hope for. Parents, especially, were conscious of their responsibility for their children and tried in every way not to draw official attention to themselves. Ordinary people went about their daily lives, trying to eke out the rations, keeping an eye on the flood of new regulations published almost daily in the newspapers or given out on the wireless. Those same newspapers showed a large measure of conformity and a new prudishness: Nazism then was an unwholesome mixture of oppression and Grundyism. The months passed.

In March 1942 the British Dominions held a conference in Ottawa; the USA and the British government-in-exile were invited to send observers. After much discussion it was decided, by a majority vote, that the status quo post bellum, however deplorable, was immutable into even the distant future. Negotiations should therefore be opened with the government of the Reich with a view to normalising relations – especially trade. The USA accepted this decision; the British exiles fought bitterly against it but were overruled. Effectively the dominions had withdrawn recognition from the exile government; after a few more months in which it issued declarations of undying defiance, this gradually faded away. Its leader, Winston Churchill, died the following year in Vancouver.

Soon after this the German government announced a

pan-European conference to be held in Berlin; its main purpose would be to regulate the state of the new Europe, especially the relationship between each of the subject states and the Reich. The conference opened in November 1942, amid great and spectacular trumpetings: torchlight processions, flags, bands, speeches by major and minor dignitories in all the countries of what was now to be clearly the Greater Reich. The delegates sat for several months. After an opening session, during which the Führer spoke for a full two hours, an agenda was drawn-up and much solid work was done. Various sub-committees were set in action and the world waited the eventual outcome with a mixture of cynicism and faint hope. Briefly, each of the occupied countries would work towards membership of a European Federal Union, acknowledging the leading role of Germany. Defence, finance and foreign affairs would be run from Berlin, under the direct control of the corresponding Reich ministry. A council of ministers was set up, in semi-permanent session, to rule on matters concerning the Union as an entity: internal trade and diplomatic representation.

By march 1943 the Federal Union (Bund Europäischer Länder) was officially acknowledged. Its constitution was so drawn-up that for the indefinite future Germany would have a decisive voice in both external and internal matters; Adolf Hitler was appointed Führer for life – on his death his successor would be appointed by 'appropriate organs of the Party' a phrase which was to cause considerable confusion and indecision in later years.

Education everywhere came closely under German scrutiny – if not, effectively, direct control. German was to be the first language in all European schools and all children were to learn it from the time they started school. From the start of the secondary stage, German was to be the medium of instruction. Crash courses were initiated and all teachers and lecturers were given a period of grace in which they had to qualify in the use of the German language, on pain of losing their jobs should they fail. For the man and woman in the street, newspapers and the wireless ran courses and these proved very popular, especially with people having direct contact with the occupying forces.

All existing youth organisations were dissolved. In their place came the Bund Freier Europäischer Jugend – the League of Free European Youth. Only in Germany did the Hitler Youth continue. All kind of international youth functions were arranged, not only in Germany but in all the federated countries, and these proved hugely successful. Undoubtedly, a big factor in this was the common language.

Scotland and Wales had been declared separate states; Ulster was permitted to join Eire, which was allowed to remain independent but could apply for membership of the Union if it wished. In fact, Eire recognised that its independence had always depended on using Britain for many of its needs and in October 1943 it adhered to the treaty of Europe.

By the spring of 1944 Britain was functioning wholly as part of the European Federation. While the man in the street seemed to have adjusted well enough to the changes, there were still signs that insularity was not wholly dead. True, there was no Resistance movement: what was there to hope or work for? Yet when the very British Promenade concerts were restored and ran their usual course (albeit with rather more German music than had been customary – though no Mendelssohn, of course), there was a significant moment.

By tradition, the last evening ended with the Fantasia of British sea-songs, terminating with the singing of 'Rule Britannia'. This time not all the audience sang and when the music reached 'Britons never, never, never shall be . . . ' the voices had faded quite away; some people looked at their feet and struggled for self-control but others wept openly. It was at that moment, said the American reporter, that many of the British realised that they had played fast and loose with history just once too often – and that the verdict of history was irrevocable. The episode was, of course, reported to the proper quarters and in future the singing of 'Rule Britannia' was banned, joining 'Jerusalem' and the National Anthem in the dustbin of history. The lesson was underlined by the consciousness that everyone within hearing of a rendering of 'Deutschland über alles' was required to stand in silence until it ended – this, together with the Nazi anthem, the Horst Wessel song.

Yet things slowly eased. The activities of the Gestapo and the SD, the effective arm of the RSHA, were no longer so apparent. Rationing had eased considerably. The mark and the pound now stood at a reasonable relationship. The lack of political activity had ceased to mean a lot – especially as Independents were allowed to stand in local and national elections, and these could air the practical grievances of their constituents. Then in mid-March 1944 came an ominous note in the press: a Soviet spy-ring had been uncovered, with branches in several countries. There had been atrocities carried out by Soviet border troops on defenceless European citizens; papers had been found, hinting at a scheme to overrun Europe. Many units of the Wehrmacht quietly left Britain, to the concern of local tradesmen. The Legion of Saint George, now at regimental strength, left its depot and moved to an unknown destination across the Channel. Its constant recruiting campaign was stepped-up. There were whispers of troop movements eastward from all the European states and an air of brooding expectation hung in the air.

On April 12th 1944 the early morning wireless opened up with military music and fanfares of trumpets: Europe had decided to defend itself against an impending Soviet attack. Before first light forces – mainly German – had crossed on a broad front into Soviet territory; the Luftwaffe was in action giving tactical support and units of the German fleet in the Baltic were bombarding unspecified targets.

Within two days the fighting was over fifty miles into Soviet territory and had soon crossed out of one-time Poland and into the USSR itself. The Wehrmacht was brutally efficient: prisoners were taken by the hundred thousand in huge encircling movements and were despatched westwards into the huge POW camps being rapidly constructed to accommodate them.

In little more than a month Leningrad was cut off from the south and the east: its only access to the hinterland was via a huge detour north of Lake Ladoga. German forces had soon reached the western outskirts of Moscow and a newsreel showed clearly men posing at a suburban tramstop. At Kursk the Russians committed their huge tank forces and after a three-day battle the Germans smashed them – largely through the accurate bombing of hundreds of Stukas under fighter cover; many of these fighters were ex-Royal Air Force Hurricanes and Spitfires, now flown by German pilots. Kiev fell; Charkow was still resisting bitterly; Djnepropetrovsk was taken, though the Russians had destroyed the extensive hydro-electric installations before retreating. Odessa was surrounded and German forces had cut-off the Crimea.

In this campaign, it was announced, five battalions of British volunteers had fought, along with similar contingents from other European states. Spain had sent the Blue Division. The German leadership paid tribute to the fighting qualities of their allies. The Balkan states, Bulgaria, Hungary and Yugoslavia, had thrown in their lot completely with the Germans and now it was an all-European army which smashed its way forward, maintaining a momentum against which the Soviets, without allies and thrown wholly on to their own resources, were unable to stabilise a fighting front. Turkey saw clear the writing on the wall and, heedless of treaty obligations, opened the Bosphorus to German naval units – among them several ships which had once been part of the French and the British navies.

By the end of August Moscow had fallen; Stalin and the Russian government had left for an undisclosed destination east of the Urals. By the end of the first week in September the Wehrmacht and its allies stood on a line from Archangel south and east along the Severnaya Dvina, to Perm and Sverdlovsk, Chelyabinsk, Orenburg and thence along the Ural to the Caspian Sea. In the rump of the Soviet Union east of this line there was hardly organised resistance or effective government.

There the fighting stopped: the invaders set to work to build a line which could be held indefinitely.

At first this line was little more than a series of strongly-defended hedgehogs at strategic points, largely supplied by air and with mobile columns patrolling between them. But there was little to fear: the Russians had lost their industry and their sources of fuel; more, they had largely lost the will to fight and many of them, especially from the Baltic republics and the Ukraine had flocked to join the German forces as auxiliaries.

On the Pacific coast the Japanese had seized Vladivostok and the coastal strip running north as far inland as Khabarovsk; they had taken the chance, also, to possess themselves of the long-disputed island of Sakhalin. What was left of the USSR, still territorially vast, was only sparsely settled, without any industry and dependent on an agricultural existence.

Europe was at last firmly and irrevocably united. The task of building a cohesive Eastern Wall was to take generations and create endless employment – especially in the steel and concrete industries. For a time, too, the armed forces would have to be maintained at a level which permitted an adequate garrison in the east. But in fact the local peasant population seemed largely to accept the situation and very soon the wary soldiers were to find that their principal activity was trading with their former enemies for food of all kinds. In imitation of Roman policy, two millennia previously, demobilised soldiers could claim large grants of land in the occupied eastern territories; those settlers would live in fortified manor houses, linked by radio with each other and with regular security forces, and could hire local labour at favourable rates. There was no shortage of applicants: gradually the East Wall stabilised.

By November 1944, with all her one-time enemies now integrated into her European empire and no potential adversary to fear, Germany felt able to relax conditions in the occupied countries of the west. A much-needed currency reform stabilised trade and industry: the Reichsmark was a standard currency and all prices everywhere were quoted in it first. In addition, each country could use its own units, at a rate laid down initially in Berlin and in time to come by the finance ministers of all the lands, meeting annually. Some foods were removed from rationing – the Ukraine now supplied massive quantities of food of all kinds and the abandonment of collective- and state-farms promised much-increased yields in time for the next winter. A massive economic plan organised with reasonable efficiency inter-European trade, to some extent eliminating the more-wasteful effects of free-for-all competition. Politically, there was progress: each country was allowed limited elections – 'limited' in the sense that while no other parties than the National Socialist Party was allowed, yet true independents might stand for election in their own countries and even be nominated to serve in the Council of Europe. In Britain, for example, this resulted in a House of Commons of 453 NS members and some 145 Independents. The Upper House had long been abolished, true to the Hitler dictum: 'There is only one aristocracy: the aristocracy of work.'

Europe was humming like a top; the conditions of life were improving steadily – even the Gestapo had lost its dreaded aura now that almost all opponents of the New Order had been eliminated. The concentration camps, whose very existence had never been officially acknowledged, were known to be gradually emptying. With so much unsettled land in the east, those Jews who had somehow survived the killings were moved out, supplied with the barest necessities for a rural economy and forcibly resettled in the one-time Turkestan, Uzbekistan and Kazakhstan. Life was hard for them but at least they now had a chance to survive.

In December of 1944 came a momentous announcement: Germany now possessed atomic bombs and the means – rockets and intercontinental bombers – to deliver them. The rest of the world was asked to believe that there was no intention whatever of using these dreadful weapons; the Führer's lifelong dream of a united Europe had now been attained and all Europe's work and planning thenceforth would be devoted to increasing prosperity and freedom within its frontiers. Those frontiers were mainly delineated by oceans, and the East Wall was just as immutable as the shore of any ocean. The rest of the world, effectively the Federated States of Greater America and the Greater East Asia Co-Prosperity Sphere, had no choice but to accept this assurance. To seal her promises of goodwill Germany proposed a meeting of the heads of state of the three great powers and in April of 1945 Geneva hosted what was, perhaps, the most important conference in the history of the world to that date. The three national leaders signed a declaration of pacific intent; in secret clauses, not to be made public for another fifty years, they divided the remainder of the world into agreed spheres of interest. The Antarctic Continent, it was agreed, would be left free of exploitation until some future date, when another meeting would address itself to the problem.

Effectively, that conference settled all political issues of any magnitude and the world could look forward to an indefinite period of peace and progress.

In July 1949 the world was rocked by the unexpected death of the Führer, Adolf Hitler. It was now announced that for some years he had been suffering from cancer and, knowing that his time was limited, had speeded up the march of events so that he would live to see his great dream fulfilled, a Europe united under German leadership. All Europe mourned the passing of its elder statesman: the 'Father of Europe', as he was now called. This simple son of a humble family in a small town in Austria had changed the face of the world, had united a continent, had personally redesigned the rebuilding of Berlin and of his home-town, Braunau. The obituaries were careful to omit any accounts of the inhuman deeds done earlier in his name, perhaps by his direct inspiration: those deeds could not be undone.

The Führer's final words: 'Hoama geganga' were a reversion to the speech of his boyhood, 'going home', and perhaps revealed the small-town petty-bourgeois so tightly concealed

128

within the world statesman. The state funeral was as grand as the mind of man could imagine – but already the struggle for the succession was in progress.

It seems, now, that the facade of Party unity concealed many conflicting ambitions among the Nazi 'Bonzen': the big shots. None was willing to stand down and attempts were made to form temporary alliances to keep this one or that one from supreme power: the position of Chancellor of the European Union and the Führer of the all-Europe NS Party. Himmler, Goering and Goebbels were the main contestants and for several days there was, apparently, desperate in-fighting behind closed doors while the nations waited for a statement. In the end a compromise was reached: none of the chief contestants would become Führer: instead the title would pass to a comparative outsider, Baldur von Schirach. At least none of the leading figures saw him as a dangerous rival and it appears now that the intention was merely to put him in as a stop-gap until one or the other saw a suitable chance to make a later bid for supreme power. As often happens, the stop-gap grew to fill the post: as Reichsjugendführer, the leader of the combined youth movement, von Schirach was known to and popular with all who had come out of the earlier Hitlerjugend and the later equivalents in the other lands of the Union. He was known to be a moderate and he had no apparent enemies.

To general surprise he proved to have some decided ideas of his own. Once all the armed forces and all the legislative assemblies of Europe had sworn the required oath of fealty to him as the new Leader, von Schirach formulated several wide-ranging decrees.

The powers of the individual states vis-à-vis the Federation, and especially, vis-à-vis Germany itself, were strengthened. The Federal Union was to acquire a second chamber composed of representatives nominated by all the states – men not necessarily from the political field alone. The new Führer wasted no time before he addressed the two houses in a joint session. It became clear that he saw Europe as a federation of equal states, with Germany no more (but no less) than primus inter pares. We had now, he pointed out, one common language, one currency, one central legislative body, one common citizenship, one economic structure. Europe was in every way a world power, so strong that no other power could weaken it in any way.

January 1st 1951 was declared to be United Europe Day and was to be observed on that day in after years throughout the Union. The celebrations were on a scale which excelled anything of the kind ever recorded. To mark the occasion further, there would be internal elections in all states on March 1st, and as soon as possible after that date there would be a chance to nominate a completely new Central Council – both houses.

Everywhere the breath of hope suffused the peoples; the bad days were over, never to return – after all, where were the enemies to be suppressed?

By mid-1951, therefore, a mere eleven years since the end of that last short European war, the world had stabilised into three great power blocks, having no cause whatever for quarrel with each other. For the first time in its history, Europe was wholly united; its people looked forward to growing prosperity and a high degree of personal freedom.

The future had begun.

As a PS to the above.

Dear David;

Here, then, is the résumé for which you asked. As I said earlier, there is much detail to fill in if you need to do so.

I have described in some detail the events in the land of your and my ancestors; there was a common saying in Britain, then, that 'It can't happen here.' This cushioned the British against unpleasant reality – until one day that reality broke through and had to be acknowledged: it *had* happened. I have long considered myself as a true European; my British ancestry is merely incidental. You, however, still resident there, may feel some

solidarity with the England which went down into unprecedented defeat. Remember, however, what I said earlier about the
two points of view, the immediate and the historical.

From time immemorial it had been British policy, from her
geographical position out on the rim, to play-off the nations of
the continent one against the other. Not so much 'divide and
rule' as 'divide and play a dominant role'. For centuries it
effectively stifled any move towards European unity. Can we
not now see, from our viewpoint in history, that defeat and
unspeakable suffering were the price for the world which we
can now enjoy and pass on to our children?

Once again, I strongly recommend to you that you read the
Weggendorf book slowly and thoughtfully; it will supply you
with a mass of detail to fill-out the outline I have provided. And,
I repeat, if you have any queries, do get into touch with me. If I
can't answer any query you may have, someone in the Faculty
certainly will. My professorship and my rank in the Party do
take up a lot of my time but I can always push things aside to
make time for my godson.

Do try to attend the Central Party Congress in July. Nürnberg
is a fascinating, mediaeval city and the pageantry is always
deeply moving. I could introduce you to several people who
could be most helpful to your career.

Sincerely,

Tom.

8

Who wins?

Who wins his love shall lose her —
Who loses her shall gain.

from the Golden Treasury of Scottish verse.

When our neighbours, Joe and Mary Dutton, told us that they were going to move, my old girl and I were very put out. The Duttons were about the last of the original families in our road and we had all been friends for many years. We used to drop in and out of each others' houses and had enjoyed several shared holidays; on Sundays we lunched alternately in this house or that. By and large we had formed a happy partnership — and now they were going to move. To be near their children and grandchildren, they told us, and this we understood though we ourselves could hardly follow their example: our son and his family now lived in Canada and our daughter even further away, in New Zealand.

During the fifteen years or so that we had lived at 'Cremona' (the old girl's choice of name) our locality had gone up in the world, both socially and financially. The nearby motorway junction had put us within easy reach of London and our situation, atop a gentle hill overlooking the upper reaches of the Thames, made the village very attractive. One by one the original families had sold out, at inflated prices, and a totally different class of resident had moved in. Our neighbour on the other side was a retired captain RN; he often spoke to me over the hedge dividing our back-gardens though his manner was always distinctly bridge-to-lower-deck. Automatically and unerringly he had classified us, and years of unquestioned authority had equipped him with a veneer of whose existence he was quite unconscious. A few doors further along the road lived a sometime-Air Commodore and opposite to him lived an ex-Brigadier. These people always made a point of addressing each other by their one-time ranks, which obviously meant a great deal to them, and they expected everyone else to do the same. The house opposite to our own was now the home of a family having unspecified connections with the world of high finance and almost every weekend their drive was jammed with expensive cars. Their occupants would often look across to our plaster pixies clustered around a brightly-painted plastic well – the OG thought they added a decent bucolic touch – and would exchange condescending smiles with each other. Meanwhile, we led our simple lives, an island of sanity amid all this new wealth and rank. And now the Duttons were to leave and we should be isolated.

Once Joe and Mary had gone we waited with considerable interest, as you might imagine, to see who would take over the vacant house. There was a constant stream of visitors and it was not long before the agent's board came down; soon a succession of workmen appeared, apparently bidden to bring the house up to a standard worthy of the new owners. It didn't look very hopeful to us: we knew that Joe and Mary had left the place in superb order and anyone who wanted more, and was willing to pay a great deal of money to get it, was hardly likely to be our kind of person. Indeed, the procession of decorators, plumbers, builders and even landscape gardeners showed that a very great deal of money was being spent, over and above the very inflated cost of the house. Yet for a long time we did not glimpse the new owners; they were represented, it seemed, by a clerk of works who turned up from time to time, spoke with various contractors and made notes on a clipboard.

One day I managed to speak to him. He was professionally vague: 'Very nice people,' he told us. 'Pots of money. Paid the purchase price cash down.'

I tell you, it did not look promising, either to the OG or to me; she was all for cashing-in on today's price, about five times as much as we had given for the house, and moving somewhere where property values were not so high – nor were the social aspirations of the neighbours. I had to admit that she might be right but, 'Hang on a bit longer,' I said. 'Let's see how things develop.' I was reluctant to leave 'Cremona' after so many years. Meanwhile, she pored over the *AA Book of the Road* , selecting possible locations and even writing away to house-agents in areas ranging from Taunton to Tunbridge Wells and from Chichester to Shrewsbury. She was sure she would win eventually and privately I felt that she probably would.

The days passed. The flow of specialists next door dwindled and stopped: apparently 'Mon Abri' was now ready for occupation. Still we waited. The old girl developed the habit of standing behind the curtains in our lounge and twitching them far enough away from the wall to permit her full observation of next door's drive; during her day she often spent the odd five minutes or so thus occupied.

Then one afternoon I was pottering around the front garden. The gnomes really needed repainting; the hedge was calling out to be clipped; it was almost time to run the mower over the lawn. Then a most imposing car drove into the drive of 'Mon Abri' and stopped. I ceased work and stared unashamedly; I saw the lounge curtain twitch and knew that the OG was on the qui vive.

A man emerged from the driving seat of the car and scurried around to the rear passenger door on the near-side; a woman got out, slowly and deliberately. In my male ignorance I registered only that she was expensively dressed; my wife would undoubtedly price for me every garment in detail – even, I wouldn't wonder, down to her underclothes. My new neighbour was of a build that I would describe, charitably, as 'stately'; not fat, you understand, but reasonably ample – something to get hold of if you were that way inclined. The estate agent, who had parked behind them, like a tug behind an ocean liner, already had the front door open and the woman entered the house. At no time did I see her face; that would have to wait. The man – her husband? – was now busily at work removing a succession of expensive suitcases from the boot. It was a large boot; there were many cases, some of them very large indeed. The poor man was in constant motion, lugging each load up the steps and into the hall, and returning for more. At last it was done; he emerged from the house, locked the boot, stretched his shoulders in relief after his exertions and looked around him. At that moment he was no more than ten yards from me and it dawned on me that his face was vaguely familiar. Then he saw me and froze; for a few seconds we looked earnestly at each other – clearly, he had recognised me.

We moved closer, eyes still scanning each other's face and suddenly I realised: it was Max. Max Maddison. We had once been close friends but had not met for, oh, some thirty years or more. During the war we had lost touch, as was common amongst servicemen posted at a few days' notice to the furthest ends of the earth. I had hardly given him a thought in recent years. I remembered all over again the Three Musketeers, as we were then called, and with a pang I thought of Jimmy Bull.

Then we were together, separated only by a low hedge. His face was lit by a broad smile.

'Pluto,' he said. 'Well, fancy that. Just fancy!'

'Well, Max,' I replied, 'it's been a long time.'

And for the moment there was nothing else to say. We stood and grinned at each other like two Cheshire cats; there was so much waiting to be said that for the moment we were mute.

At that moment the agent came out of the house, ignored Max, climbed into his car and drove off. The woman appeared in the doorway now minus her furs.

'Maxwell,' she called imperiously. 'Come on now. There's a lot to do.'

The smile vanished from Max's face; he seemed to cringe slightly. He turned to her.

'Look, dear,' he replied. 'See who's living next door.'

At first it seemed that she would brush this aside and order him to his duties but then curiosity overcame her and she came

135

down the steps towards us – and it was Lena. Unmistakeably Lena. The years had brought out a distinct querulousness but then her face lit in a smile of genuine warmth.

'Pluto!' she said; she leaned over the hedge and I did the same and kissed her. The old nickname, so long unused, evoked a flood of memories and feelings. Then I realised that the OG would be bursting with curiosity behind her twitching curtain and that in fairness I must get her out to share in the proceedings. I said, 'Hang on a moment. I'll fetch my wife.'

I turned and went quickly into the house. The old girl had come to meet me as I entered; she was, clearly, bursting with questions. Before the dam could burst I said, forcefully, 'Come outside. I want to introduce you to some old friends.'

Uncomprehending but patting her hair to rights, she followed me. The two women eyed each other; obviously, they were already on terms of armed neutrality.

'I don't know which way around I should say this,' I announced. (I am never good at protocol and it seems to be oddly important to many people otherwise-sensible). 'Anyway, Lena, this is my wife Pat. Pat: this Lena and Max. We were all friends, back in the days before the war.'

Lena looked mildly uncomfortable.

'Well, actually,' she pointed out, 'everyone calls me Helena, these days. Anyway, I'm glad to know you.'

My old girl murmured something conventional and the two shook hands; the armed neutrality was still there, I could see. There would have to be an inquest later. Then Pat and Max shook; this time there was a genuine smile on both sides; Max was still, after all this time, a great charmer.

It was soon generally agreed that the time was hardly right for a prolonged catching-up just then, so with fervent promises to get together again very shortly we all turned away and returned to our respective homes. Even as we shut the front door, the old girl had started.

'You never told me . . . ' but I cut her short.

'Please go and make some tea, dear, and I'll tell you all about it.'

She gave me a suspicious look but went into the kitchen; I sat in the lounge and mustered my memories, preparing for a lengthy session. My mind was pushing open doors which had remained closed these many years and old emotions – love, fear, regret – were stirring again.

Everybody used to call us the Three Musketeers; we spent all our free time together and even at work two of us were never far apart except when we were flying. Of course, all this was a long time ago: half an incredible century ago, and now . . . But I wonder what would have become of the original Three Musketeers had they grown through maturity and into age. There's a novel there, waiting to be written – but not by me.

Anyway, to resume: Max and I really revolved around Jimmy Bull, planets to his sun, as it were. He was tallish, dark, with a mass of brown curls clustered thickly to his scalp. His accent was genuine cut-glass and his antecedents, of which he rarely spoke, were wholly different from those of the rest of us, plebs through and through. Why he was in the ranks was a mystery. I did ask him once and derived a confused impression that it was a gesture of revolt, though against whom was unclear – his superior-bourgeois upbringing, perhaps. I know that our officers were mildly puzzled by an aircraftsman who was so obviously officer-material; in the pre-war RAF the commissioned ranks were invariably drawn from a stratum marked out by accent. We plebs spoke anything from the argot of the larger conurbations from which many of us came, to the burr of many outlying parts of Britain. As a system of selection it seemed to work well enough in a rough and ready fashion, though of course it was wasteful of much potential talent. The war was to change that, to some extent at least.

Max spoke the modified Cockney of well-to-do South Croydon; he was placid and inclined to reticence but there was something about him which was most attractive to women. He made full use of that talent, I can tell you, though a current girl-friend usually lasted at most three weeks. For him the fun

137

lay in the chase; pursuit was ecstatic but possession merely static. He told me once that women were like chewing-gum and left me to work out the meaning for myself.

Oddly, the third member of the group was myself; 'oddly' because there was no apparent reason why I should have been drawn into their company. My accent was mildly north-country and to their sophistication I could oppose only acute shyness based on a huge lack of self-confidence. Even today I cannot see why they allowed me to trail around with them but they did and I was grateful.

Max was an instrument-basher and so did not fly; Jimmy and I were wireless operator/gunners and totally hooked on flying. We realised, of course, that in 1938 war was not only inevitable but imminent and that then our jobs would become overnight very dangerous indeed but we refused to worry and simply enjoyed each day as it came.

The joys had necessarily to be simple and inexpensive; for each of us pay was rather less than four shillings – twenty pence – a day. Payday was Thursday, so at the weekends we would be comparatively flush. On the Friday evening we would visit one of the two local cinemas and on the way back to the camp stop off at the Wayside Caff (sic) for supper; on the Saturday we would wander down to the 'Crown', order our initial drinks (for me a half-pint of mild ale which would usually last me for the evening) and go through to the small and crowded hall at the rear. Here there would be a small local band giving out, *ff*, the hits of the moment, while on the minuscule dance-floor couples would gyrate, lit fitfully by a revolving, many-faceted overhead globe. I would sit at one of the small tables, holding the fort for my two friends while they circulated, chatting-up the local talent.

Before long they would return, usually with a girl each in tow. There would be introductions which I always found mildly embarrassing: I could never plug-in to the kind of persiflage which had replaced or displaced conversation. From time to time my friends would take to the floor again but later in the evening, having decided that an outlay of a couple of Babychams (the

138

apparent nectar of local womanhood, it appeared) would be a reasonable gamble, all four would vanish for perhaps half an hour. Later the men would return, usually alone. I envied their self-assurance, their techniques of seduction, their total sophistication. In their absence I watched the dancers, humming to myself the ditties given out by the band: 'Music, maestro, please,' 'That old feeling,' 'Deep Purple,' and the others. Even today the mere mention of the titles is enough to make me long to re-live a time so irrevocably gone. Passing friends would stop for a casual chat and then at last we three would leave the smoke-impregnated racket and walk slowly back to camp.

As we ambled my friends would discuss their conquests of the evening, often in terms which aroused in me only frustrated lust and then we would check-in again at the guardroom.

Sunday was a kind of montage of bodies lying in bed at all kinds of hours; non-stop Radio Luxemburg; countless sheets of newsprint littering the floor; endless games of brag. By the evening I would smarten myself up to attend Evensong in the local church while my two friends would probably have to borrow from me enough money to supply themselves with supper at the Naafi. A few more small loans would then tide them over the next days until payday again brought the golden eagle, as the saying had it. Usually such loans were paid back but sometimes Jimmy would be over-committed. Then he would make his apologies and tell me that I would be repaid amply 'when my money arrives.'

It appeared, if he could be believed, that Bull père, deceased in obscure circumstances, had been engaged in the lucrative business of smuggling arms into China from bases in Hong Kong and Macao. After his death a great deal of money had been frozen in a bank somewhere in that region and various protracted legal processes were needed before it could be released. Jimmy was the sole heir. He did not explain why there was no mother to claim her share and we did not like to ask: it might well have overtaxed his powers of invention or ours of credulity. I wrote off such occasional losses against the joy I had in their company and my gratitude to them both in accepting me into their companionship.

A time came when Max's latest conquest, Lena, refused persistently to be shaken off as so many others had been previously. She was quite besotted with Max and made no secret of it. He quickly lost all interest: for him, novelty was all. Yet she refused to leave us. Every Saturday found her at our table, even buying her own drinks and occasionally standing treat for the other two. I was, as I have said, no great boozer and my aim was to get through each such evening with the minimum consumption of alcohol. And Jimmy was totally enamoured of her; he tried every weapon in his armoury to arouse her interest, but to no avail: she would not be averted. I was fascinated to mark the byplay between the three of them. As a matter of fact, I was becoming increasingly far gone on Lena, myself, though in the company of my two friends of course there could be no hope for such as me, so I kept my mouth shut and tried not to look at her too obviously. Later, on our way home, Max bewailed his inability to scrape her off despite the succession of other girls which he paraded in front of her – and went out of the room with, for the usual half-hour.

Then one afternoon I came back to the billet; it was midweek and I was expecting no more of the evening than that we should eat at the Naafi, at my expense, and play the odd hand of crib. As I came in Jimmy was sitting on the edge of his bed; his face bore a serious look and in one hand he clasped a large white envelope. Max sat opposite him, equally quiet and serious. The tableau was intriguing: what could have happened?

'Come on, then,' I asked. 'What's up?'

Both of them looked up at me. Jimmy said, 'It's come at last.' And held out the envelope.

'What's come?'

'The money. Look.'

He held out the envelope, opened the flap and half-withdrew a thick wad of papers: five-pound notes. He peeled off two of them and handed them to me.

'I must owe you that at least,' he said. 'You're welcome to them now.'

It was my turn to look stunned. I unfolded those lovely crackling fivers – the old kind, large and white and inscribed in beautiful copperplate.

'But . . . ' I started and then stopped: the situation was too much to take in. One or two of the other inhabitants of the room hovered near, looking on with awe. Jimmy suddenly looked around.

'Drinks for you all tonight, on me,' he announced. 'At the Crown. Seven o'clock.'

There was a general cheer followed by a rapid dispersal as men went back to their bedspaces to get out their civilian clothes: it was not done to leave camp in uniform. This evidently promised to be an evening to remember.

Max had hardly taken his eyes off that envelope. When Jimmy made his offer he merely looked startled.

'It would be to-bloody-night,' he complained. He looked up and for the first time he noted my presence. 'I'm on fire picquet at six o'clock. Well,' bitterly, 'I hope you all have a smashing time.'

Then a thought struck him; he looked me full in the face.

'Tell you what. You don't drink much. I suppose you wouldn't . . . '

'All right, all right,' I replied. 'I'll stand in for you. If you've already blancoed your webbing I'll need it: there's no time to do my own and that sod Elliot is duty sergeant.'

His face lit up. With more fervour than he had ever shown before he said, 'Ta, mate. Any time I can do anything for you, *anything*, just let me know.'

'That's OK,' I replied. 'Now I'd better go across and get some tea. Just put out your kit on my bed before you go out. Don't get too boozed up.'

There was some fervent back-slapping and, rather bashfully, I took my eating-irons and wandered across to the cookhouse. In truth, I would not miss the booze-up, though fire picquet

141

was a drag. By the time I got back to the billet my friends had left, as had most of the other occupants of the room. A few stragglers were putting the finishing touches – mostly with Brylcreem – to their appearance and as I left for the guardroom to commence duty, they also left to book out for the evening.

By 6 am my duty ended and I went directly to the cookhouse for an early breakfast. I guessed what state the billet would be in and was in no hurry to renew acquaintance with the general squalor. Some time after seven I entered the billet and it was as I had expected. Clothing was strewn over the floor and there was a smell of vomit; two beds had not been slept in: the ten–ants were presumably adrift. I went over and woke Max; he opened his eyes, squinted blearily at me, grunted and asked, 'Wossatime?'

'About seven-thirty. Out that pit, intrepid bird-man.'

He groaned, shut his eyes again and was motionless. I went over to Jimmy and shook his shoulder. As he stirred into pre-wakefulness I said, 'Want to buy a battleship? Or we have a very good selection of used tramcars.'

His brow furrowed; his eyes opened and he stared uncompre-hending. Then full consciousness returned and he, too, groaned. His hands went up to his head. I grinned unsympathetically and as I turned away noticed the envelope: there seemed to be one solitary fiver left out of the fifty or so which had been there the previous evening. Clearly, it had been a great, if expensive, night.

Now the room came slowly and painfully to life; despite the groans there was agreement that it had been a 'wizard' evening. As always, I was baffled by their idea of 'wizard', in view of the aching heads and bleary eyes.

Most evenings now Jimmy set out with the renewable wodge of notes, accompanied by Max; one night he returned driving a large and imposing metallic-turquoise car – even grander than the car of the Station Commander. It was some days be-fore the gate guard could restrain themselves from saluting automatically as the car turned in to the camp.

The following weekend the Flight Commander flew down to an aerodrome on the South Coast for some kind of celebration; I went with him in order to maintain radio contact. We arrived in time for lunch on the Saturday and I was bidden to amuse myself until after lunch the following day. In those days it never even occurred to me to resent such a state of affairs; ours but to do and, as was soon to turn out, die.

About teatime on the Sunday I bowled into the billet; it must have been some ten days since Jimmy had come in to his money. I was suddenly struck by the changed appearance of my friends. But that was soon to alter: the previous evening they had returned to camp totally incapable and had been spotted by the Orderly Officer. The following Monday morning they appeared, caps off, in front of the CO and were awarded – a comical term – a week's 'jankers': confined to camp. This was unpleasant but at least it enforced a practically alcohol-less week and by the following Monday they both looked distinctly healthier.

Then came a Saturday when we three, as of old, sat at a table beside the dance-floor. With financial prosperity my two friends had taken to drinking rum but I resisted all their persuasions and stuck to my half-pint of ale. Once again Lena materialised but now, I noticed, she was marginally more responsive to Jimmy's wooing. Soon the two of them rose and joined the crowd on the floor; Max, unusually, opted to sit it out.

'She seems to be fonder of Jimmy these days,' I offered.

'Your nose is out of joint, that's pretty obvious.'

'It was never *in* joint. It's taken me weeks to get rid of her. Jimmy will do fine.' He eyed the writhing couples, lit fitfully by that revolving and many-faceted globe.

'You mean, she's seen there's nothing doing, at last?' I enquired.

'She should have seen that weeks ago. Anyway, there are a lot of reasons now why Jimmy is a better prospect. Almost a quarter of a million reasons.' He looked at me with a faint smile parting his lips. It took me a second or two to twig.

143

'As much as that?' Incredulously.

'Just about. He showed me a letter from his solicitor. It's a relief not to have her mooning over me: I wouldn't touch her with yours.' Pause. 'You're a bit sweet on her yourself, aren't you?'

I was mildly confused. 'Well, sort of.'

'You're better off without her' he said. 'She isn't . . . ' but whatever else he meant to say had to be postponed as the other two arrived back at the table. There was some lively but trivial conversation in which I took little part and soon we left for the camp, riding in that beautiful car and dropping off Lena at her home en route. I was mildly envious: money, a car, Lena: nothing like that would ever come my way. Yet I didn't begrudge Jimmy his good fortune.

During the next few weeks our activities doubled: bombing, air-firing, low-flying. (More than once some heedless farm worker had to throw himself to the ground as we roared at 200 mph, at a height of some ten feet or so, across a peaceful field.) The war was getting nearer with each day. I hardly noticed the news of the engagement of Jimmy and Lena, together with the date of the impending wedding: in view of the situation there was no time to be lost.

So one Saturday afternoon we all met at the parish church. The twenty-four inhabitants of our room turned out in best blue with webbing belts and formed a guard of honour as the bride and groom left the church; the reception was, of course, at the functions room of the Crown. I tried not to look directly at Lena at any time and eventually the couple were driven away on a four-day honeymoon – all the time that could be granted. Then I, too, slipped away; there was nothing in the reception for me. By the time the other revellers arrived back at the room I was deeply asleep and not all their noisy reminiscences availed to awaken me.

But at nineteen you are very resilient. I told myself that Lena had never been more than a hopeless twinge and even managed to believe it – in part, anyway. So I put the whole thing out of my mind. Soon Jimmy was back and the old unity was restored – during working hours, at least. For the moment Lena had gone back to her parents' home; further plans would be made once the international situation sorted itself out.

One Friday, I suppose it must have been the 1st of September, there was a massive panic. It was feared that the Luftwaffe might launch a pre-emptive strike, destroying our aircraft on the ground before a declaration of war would have ensured their dispersal to safer areas. At all RAF stations within a hundred miles of the South or East coasts aircraft took off and landed at isolated fields, designated for this purpose months in advance. Three of our kites and their crews, including Jimmy and myself, were carefully hidden under the elm-trees surrounding a large field somewhere in Oxfordshire; in those days we needed no such luxuries as runways: a short stretch of reasonably-level grass was sufficient to permit us to operate. A brittle excitement had seized us all; what would war be like and would it really come to that?

The following Sunday morning we knew the answer to the second of those questions; the answer to the first was a little longer in coming.

As it soon became evident that the skies over Britain were not to be darkened by fleets of enemy bombers – or at least, not yet – we soon gave up our dispersal and returned to base. At once Jimmy shot off, illicitly, to see Lena; he soon returned and told us that it had been decided that she should go to live with an aunt who lived at a comfortable distance from any conceivable military target. She might even be pregnant: it was still too early to say. At any rate, it was wiser in every way for her to be found a home in the heart of Radnorshire. Fortunately, there would be no financial problems; after the prodigalities of the first week or two, Jimmy had been persuaded to seek advice about farming-out his money, too, in a safe place and there would be a steady and very comfortable income.

The night before Lena was due to leave, the Three Musketeers had what might well be their last-ever meeting; in view of the occasion, it was held in a local hotel. We men sat ourselves at a table and Jimmy rose to escort his wife into the room. Lena, I could not but notice, shot one quick glance at Max and then looked away. She did not look directly at me but the sight of her, I found with an angry disgust, was still enough to cause in me a stab somewhere around the solar plexus. I had thought, and hoped, that all such nonsense was finished; I reacted by becoming even more taciturn than usual. Jimmy was obviously depressed by the coming separation; only Max was his usual carefree self. Altogether, the evening was not really a success. Even Max gave up trying to raise our spirits and soon he concentrated on drinking.

Later Jimmy drove the two of us back towards the camp, stopping the car safely short of the guardroom before turning around for a last night with Lena. When the next such would be, none of us would dare predict.

And so the war came to us. Our masters, it soon became evident, had not realised the limited capabilities either of our aircraft or of ourselves; in the process of playing themselves in they caused the RAF to squander far too many machines and crews. It was several months before sanity established itself. Most squadrons then switched to a purely night-bombing role, though our own was mainly used in daylight with occasional nocturnal forays. The daylight forays were expensive. One by one my circle of close friends contracted and new faces appeared to replace them. It was, we knew, only a question of time for all of us, though by common if tacit consent this grim prospect was never mentioned neither in public nor in private conversation. For myself, I had no hope of immortality: why should I refuse what so many of my friends had already accepted uncomplainingly?

> Lo, some we loved, the loveliest and best
> By Time and Fate of all their Vintage prest,
> Have drunk their Cup a Round or two before,
> Then, one by one, crept silently to Rest.

A determined fatalism helped, I found.

Max suddenly found himself a corporal and, only days later,

a sergeant; he left our overcrowded barrack-room (now housing no less than 28 of us) for better quarters. Jimmy and I were thrown together rather more as the comfortable, happy routine of our lives disintegrated. The other occupants of the room – fitters, riggers and other tradesmen – obviously viewed us with sympathy, shown in many insignificant ways, but by an ironclad law they never alluded to our dwindling expectation of days to come.

Then, wholly unanticipated, the blow fell. Or was it indeed a blow? One morning I was summoned to the medical block for a routine aircrew medical. It was all very old-hat: I stood or sat, blew into things, climbed on and off chairs as so often before. Then came the hearing test; a pair of earphones was put over my head and each ear was tested for acuity and frequency-response. The right ear was tested and the phones were reversed, and then there was a hold-up in the proceedings and, lost in my private thoughts, I waited patiently. The earphones were removed and the MO looked seriously at me.

'For several seconds,' he said, 'I've been testing your left ear. You have practically no hearing in it at all. Your flying days are over.'

I gaped at him; the news was too great to take in. My whole way of life was finished; what was there left? Yet the war had suddenly receded: in some kind of non-flying job I now had an excellent chance of survival.

'You are to stop flying immediately,' ordered the MO. 'I'll ring your CO and tell him. You must report to your Orderly Room at once. And do cheer up: there are quite enough men left for us to win the war without you.'

I was too dazed to see anything more than, 'Yes, sir,' so I put on my cap and, mightily confused, left for the hangar.

My friends congratulated me on the development, as did Jimmy; there was an immediate pretence that in one way or another I had squared the MO. The Flight Commander looked at me compassionately; he assumed, wrongly, that my feelings

147

about such a change of fortune must be the same as his own would have been. It was decided that I would do various odd jobs around the Section until a more-permanent job, somewhere, could be found for me. The 'Odd Jobs' were more than enough to fill my days and often a large part of my nights as well. The wonder was how we had managed to get along this far without an extra bod to help out.

Then came the night I have never forgotten, nor ever shall. We were to send out three aircraft to join a small gaggle drawn from several squadrons in the Group. The target was somewhere in north-west Germany. I was duty signaller that night. By dusk a long line of goose-neck flares were flickering smokily across the drome. I set up the flashing beacon with the code letters of the period and then I joined the Duty Pilot, the electrician and the runner at the base of the flare-path.

The first kite came waddling out and identified itself; on an order of the DP I flashed it a green light: clear to take-off. He swung into wind, opened up the engines with a roar (we turned our backs and held our hats on our heads against the blast) and accelerated down the flares. By the time he was off the ground he was invisible to us; only his navigation lights showed his position and once he had reached a reasonable height they would be switched-off. The second machine followed him. Then came the third; this, I knew, was O-Orange and in it were Jimmy and his crew. Once again I flashed a green and added a little prayer; the kite climbed away into the darkness. We turned to put out our lights and collect our kit: by the time they returned there would be enough daylight for them to land without our aid.

Then came the dreaded sound of an engine misfiring. We turned and peered through the dark. The lights of O-Orange indicated that he was slowly rolling to port, then they dipped and vanished as the kite slammed into the ground, somewhere not far from the aerodrome boundary. There was a flash and the usual composite clatter, borne to us on the moderate breeze. There was a second enormous flash, followed by a bang and a rumble as the bombs exploded; the blast was enough to remove all our hats and to drive dust stingingly into our faces as we gaped. The wreck burned fiercely.

Then followed the usual panic noises as the blood waggon and the fire tender set off on their hopeless errand. I stood without moving and without thinking; Jimmy had gone from us. The blow was numbing, too intense for conscious emotion: that would come later. The Duty Pilot spoke, thoughtfully: 'You know, you have to have a very strong constitution to walk away from a prang like that.' It was a superb example of the kind of extempore stiff-upper-lippery which was expected of us in those days: when there is nothing practical to be done, seal-off the suffering with a wisecrack. Then, automatically, we got on with our various jobs, assembling bits and pieces for towing away or for transport to the hangar.

By the time I returned to the billet the news had already gone before; although it was long after midnight, everyone was awake. Faces looked at me compassionately and a voice said, 'Bloody shame about Jimmy.' I did not reply but undressed in silence and got into bed. Someone put out the lights. Max and I met the following evening and rekindled a spark, at least, of the old companionship. We both knew, as we reminded each other, that we had been mere planets revolving around Jimmy but we knew that even that was a lot to have in common. We talked – 'Do you remember when . . . ' and even I drank too much, and on the way back to the camp in the darkness we might even have shed the odd tear. Certainly, I did.

There had to be a funeral, of course, even though what went into the coffins would have borne little resemblance to the men we had known. The pilot's body was then transported to his home village in Sussex; the other two men were buried in 'our' corner of the local churchyard; there were already too many graves there, each with its uniform headstone. Even in death, there was the bond of a common uniform. Lena was pale but brave; we exchanged a few artificial words before the ceremony and met again later at the Station Hotel. The occasional train thundering past sounded remarkably like an aircraft and I saw Lena flinch more than once. There was an air of strain and before too long Max and I, pleading duty, rose and left.

'Don't forget,' she said, as we were leaving, 'you'll always be welcome. Do keep in touch. If you have a few days' leave you can spare, come over our way. We've plenty of room and rationing has never been heard of in an area like ours. It's very beautiful: hills, woods and sheep. There's a church, a village school, a post-office and general store, a pub, a few cottages and that's the lot. I can drive down and pick you up at Knighton station. You really would be welcome.'

I thanked her and expressed interest in a possible visit, though I had no real intention of squandering any of my previous leave in that way: my home and my family had the first and only claim on any free time that came along. Max said much the same kind of thing as I although, now I come to think of it, he sounded as if he half-intended to keep his vague promise to visit her some time.

Then we were away, Max and I, walking back up the lane to the camp; we had refused offers of a lift. We spoke little. On my part I was wondering about an imminent posting; in those days the RAF had stations everywhere in the world and there was now every chance that I should be able to fulfil the exhortation of the old sweats: 'Get your knees brown', a reference to the kind of station where shorts were the normal wear.

Just as we reached the guardroom I asked Max, 'Will you really visit her?'

'I may,' he replied. 'Will you?'

'No. For me that's all over.' And we parted.

Only a few weeks later I was posted away to a station in Yorkshire; I was second in charge of a ground station, which meant that I automatically became a corporal, living in better quarters and being paid more money than when I had been flying. Moreover, at the end of a probationary period, six months or so, I should qualify for my third tape. Life was looking up. Max and I exchanged occasional letters and in this way I was kept posted with the news of the loss of several more old friends. Soon the names he mentioned were strange to me: the old timers had all been used up. As, of course, I would have been, had I not been taken off flying. Once he mentioned, briefly, a few days spent visiting Lena, but he made nothing very much of it and I forgot about it almost as soon as I had read it. So it came as a surprise when, well within the year after Jimmy's funeral, he wrote to tell me that he and Lena were to be married. Within a fortnight came an expensively-printed invitation to the wedding, together with an accompanying note to tell me that I was expected to attend, however I wangled it. A room would be available at the local hotel and I was to be at the stag-night – or else.

And so, one afternoon in mid-April of 1940 I alighted from a local train in a small country station; around were gently rolling hills, largely wooded, separated by endless fields across which sheep, small grey lice, wandered erratically. The engine wheezed and hissed; milk-churns clattered; a hoarse voice shouted something unintelligible. Then the engine shot jets of steam at ankle height across the platform; the couplings clanked and with an immense chuntering the train drew out. I went through the barrier and there were Lena and Max, standing beside the car of which Jimmy had been so proud. After the gap of several months, conversation was rather restrained. I found that I was still shy in Lena's presence. Soon I was unpacking with instructions to be down in the bar promptly at seven o'clock.

At that time, decently attired in civvies (officially forbidden by my leave-form, my 295), I found Max surrounded by several strangers – all of course male. There were introductions which only confused me. The programme was simple: tank-up largely and eat moderately. I found a quiet corner, nursed my glass of mild ale and tried to conceal boredom. Why had I come all this way? What could I have expected but ennui? There was much noisy hilarity; games involved stomping around, with selected victims consuming non-stop enormous quantities of beer. Sometimes the revellers sang – often the pornographic ditties

151

of the RAF which the local men apparently learned immediately. The door to our room was firmly closed but even so I was
mildly surprised that nobody came to remonstrate about the
words which must have been audible in the bar beyond – words
which never before, surely? had been heard in those bucolic
surroundings.

Later Max contrived to detach himself from the revellers and
came and sat beside me. 'Thank you for coming,' he said.
'You're the only link with the old days.' We both knew whom
was meant by 'the old days'. I said, and even meant, all the
conventional phrases expressive of goodwill and for a time we
sat silently, watching the jollity.

'I thought,' I said, 'I thought you were never very keen on
Lena.' It was an implied question. 'So it was quite a surprise. I
do hope it all works out well.'

By now Max had drunk a great deal of every variety of alcohol – enough to overcome somewhat his usual reserve.

'Ah,' he replied. 'But there are reasons. Almost two hundred thousand of them.' He smiled at me and gently rubbed
the side of his nose with the index finger of his right hand,
a gesture of his which I remembered well. He waited for my
response. The frankness was startling; I knew not what to
say.

'Well,' he said in self-extenuation, 'she was never keen on
Jimmy, was she? Not until . . . But she married him. She
always carried a torch for me, you know. Only a few nights
before she married him we . . . Ah well, water under the
bridge, I suppose. Anyway, she can hardly be surprised if I do
exactly what she did.'

Then he was silent. I suspected that his usual caution was
trying to fight its way through the fog of alcohol, to avoid any
further revelations, though the greatest revelation had already
been made.

I was spared the necessity of framing an impossible answer to
all this: a group of drunken louts tumbled over to our corner,
lifted him bodily from his chair and carried him over to the bar.

There one man hacked off his tie and another poured a pint of beer, with great deliberation, over his head. I sidled out, trying not to draw attention to my defection. From my bedroom I could still hear faintly the sound of distant revels.

The ceremony took place the following day. It was to be the second marriage that afternoon and there were two more couples waiting for us to finish and leave; rather a conveyor-belt system, I thought. The reception later took place in an air of forced jollity – or perhaps it was only myself who had to force the atmosphere. I declined a request that I should make a speech and as soon as I could, I left. I kissed the bride for the first time that day and as we drew apart she said earnestly, 'Now, you will keep in touch, won't you?'

I said, 'Yes', but could not have said whether I meant it or not; lap of the gods, I thought. Who knows where the war will take me – or Max? I was annoyed with myself; unworthy emotions were forcing their way into my consciousness: greed and envy. Greed – all that money, more than I would earn in a whole lifetime; envy – first I had had to watch Lena being married to Jimmy (though I hardly begrudged *him*) and now I had to see Lena married again, this time to Max. Why was I never on the receiving end of such monumental favours, I wondered. I suppressed these thoughts and eventually managed to sleep. The following day there were some goodbyes, which I privately intended to be very final ones, and then I was on my way back again.

As it happened I had been back on the station only another month when my next posting came through: east of Suez. I wrote to Max, to inform him; perhaps our paths would cross somewhere or at some time – the war brought sad partings and strange meetings. Any possible letter failed to reach me in my subsequent moves; soon I was in Egypt and then I found myself caught up by the tides of war which took me first to Algiers and later to Italy and to Malta. I never heard from Lena or Max again.

And then the years peeled off suddenly that afternoon as I

recognised an older and unfamiliar Max, toiling up the steps, festooned with luggage. Surely, that oversized, overdressed and hard faced woman could not be Lena?

But it was.

All this, of course, took a long time to tell and even so my narrative was necessarily much more condensed than I have related it here. Once or twice the OG was about to interrupt with a question, I could see, but each time I gestured her to silence. Once I had begun, I did not want to lose my thread in her investigation of side-issues; nor did I want to be coerced into protestations of undying affection now addressed to a much-worthier recipient. Affection, loyalty and gratitude would have to be taken as read. When, however, I had obviously done and sat there with my eyes still misted with memory, it was clear to me that several questions were struggling for simultaneous utterance. The one that came first was obviously the one that meant the most to her.

'Well, now you've seen her and heard her, what do you think? You were sweet on her once.'

I fielded that one easily enough though I felt a right hypocrite and was grateful that none of my friends, male, were listening. At least, I did not descend to mawkishness.

'What about our plans to move?' (*Our* plans, indeed: who had filled the house with brochures?). Anyway, I stalled on that one, being highly evasive though still, I congratulated myself, diplomatic. The OG could see – easily see – that I was not going to be pinned down and it was clear that her plans were based on the old saying about constant dripping wearing away a stone. It was a saying that she knew well – and applied often. There was a short silence and then the most practical question so far: 'As they must be upside-down, shall we invite them over for a meal tonight?'

It was the kind of question, pitched at me in the kind of way, which strongly suggested that the answer had to be 'yes'. I could see that part of her motive was disinterested neighbourliness, yet she was still full of curiosity and wanted to do more probing

154

– this time, directly. Thirty-odd years of marriage had brought us to the point where our reading of each other's mind, based on the merest semi-tone of variation in voice, bordered on straight telepathy; the actual words counted for little. So I thanked her for her kind thought and went next door to convey the invitation. The OG, already muttering purposefully to herself, made a beeline for the freezer cabinet.

The invitation was, of course, accepted; I detected in Lena (sorry, Helena) much the same curiosity as had motivated my wife. So that evening we foregathered around a table laid with the best of everything we possessed: napery, cutlery, glasses, Uncle Arthur's dinner service, which came out only on high days and holidays. I saw Lena look appraisingly around the room, mentally pricing everything from the soft furnishings to the table lay-out – even to Pat's evening gown, bought a year ago and at inordinate cost for a masonic dinner.

Conversation flowed easily enough, though Max and I dominated it. The two women were plainly just waiting. Max, I now saw, had put on flesh, though not excessively. Indeed, in that respect, who was I to comment? Yet his face showed rather more lines than I might have expected, especially in one with absolutely no financial troubles. He seemed aged beyond his years, even more reticent that he had been years ago when it came to voicing an opinion – and when he did do this, he usually darted a glance at his wife. In the course of the meal the two women seemed to thaw towards each other and eventually they both rose from the table, loaded the trolley and vanished towards the kitchen. ('It's quite all right, really. I'll just leave them until the morning.' 'No, I must help. You've been so kind to us that I'd feel guilty if I didn't give a hand.') I had no doubt what the main topic of conversation would be between them: well, my conscience was reasonably clear.

Max and I were at last left to talk freely; the door to the kitchen was firmly shut, no doubt with a view to creating conditions under which they could speak freely to each other about their respective husbands.

155

We were silent for a time; then 'It's been a long time,' I offered; banal, I admit, but it was meant to be a sighting shot, merely.

'Yes; if only Jimmy were here to join us.' Then there was silence while each of us thought back to – I almost said, 'the good years.' But we had been young and carefree and happy as of right – good years indeed. Now Max loosened up; as in years gone by, alcohol loosened his tongue.

'It's no cop, you know,' he offered suddenly. 'She knows why I married her and she doles out every pound. Everything's in her name – the house, the car – and when she gets annoyed I come in for the rough side of her tongue.'

There was a pause; I could find no words with which to answer him. Sympathy? Encouragement? Stiff-upper-lippery? With his eyes on his liqueur glass he said slowly, almost as if to himself, 'We get on well enough, in a sort of a way, I suppose. Probably no worse than many other couples. But sometimes I think she regrets marrying me. She has never said so. In front of other people we try to put on the act but when we get back home later, I'll be compared to you.'

There was another pause; from the kitchen we could hear the faint jingle of cutlery and muffled voices.

'You had the best of it, you know' he said. 'You and Pat have a real partnership. You're not a kind of lap-dog. Maxwell this and Maxwell that.' There was bitterness, now, and then he was quiet for a spell; I was very conscious that I had not yet spoken but he had left me no opening that I could see, and in any case he seemed to be venting a long-felt hurt.

'Couldn't you get a divorce?' I asked.

He looked at me; his face showed a faint tinge of – could it be despair?

'Oh, I've thought about that. But you forget, we're both RCs and even today that's important to both of us. In any case she would never give me grounds. If I did move out for two years – is it? – what would I live on until a settlement came through? No, divorce is no answer.' Again he was silent, then a flicker of the old Max came through. 'Murder, perhaps. I wonder where that rates in the league-table of sins, relative to divorce.' He smiled slightly. Then whatever else he meant to say had to be postponed: the women returned with coffee and cups, and the small talk began again.

At ten-thirty our guests excused themselves: 'it's been a long day and there's so much to do tomorrow', and left. We stood on the front porch and waved to them as they walked down the drive, then we turned and went back into the lounge.

As my OG sat down I suddenly felt gratitude and a stirring of affection; I leaned forward and kissed her cheek.

'Oh,' suspiciously. 'And what's that for? You can't have been up to anything yet. Are you trying to make up for chances yet to come?'

She's nobody's fool, is my OG, and she never fails to work out all the angles.

'Nothing like that,' I replied, and smiled across at her. 'It's just that I've realised how lucky I am.'

She received this dead-pan; she was still suspicious – then her expression changed again as she worked out another possible angle.

'Well, we're not going to have any of that old nonsense tonight, either. You aren't going to get around me. Time you had more sense.'

'Nothing like that in my mind,' I reassured her. 'It was just as I said, honestly.' And I smiled again.

Even so, she was wary; perhaps I should have been in the habit of showing more overt affection: perhaps I would in the future. Well, perhaps: mustn't spoil them, you know. Soon we retired.

She had her way; we moved, barely a month later. I could not bear to live alongside a defeated and subjugated Max. We exchanged promises to keep in touch – even to exchange visits in the unspecified future, but soon all that was left was the regular Christmas card with the briefest of reports inside.

There's more than one way of winning, I had learned.

9

A Fairy Story for Christmas, and quite unsuitable for Children: by R P, with the unwitting co-operation of

E Brown	Bismark
The Bard	T S Eliot
W Disney	J E Flecker
John Keats	F Cornford
Dr Johnson	Lord Byron
W H Davies	Marshall MacMahon

When we come to the end of a . . .

'Bugger,' spat the fairy, with considerable feeling. And who can blame her? It was an expression often on the lips of passing gardeners; she did not know the meaning of the expression but it was, she had found, efficacious to express anger or frustration or even hatred. From where she sat, in the branches of some kind of conifer, she was surrounded by some of the very finest god-wottery in the kingdom but to her the immediate outlook was unrelievedly bleak. Weltschmerz took her by the throat and momentarily irritation was drowned in self-pity. No time to stand and stare, that was her trouble; not that there were any sheep or cows in the Gardens. All that unpaid overtime the previous evening with an odious little girl who had made all the right wishes and done all the right things and who had to have those wishes gratified even though it was long past the hours laid down in the Catering Wages Act. Nasty little creep. She had a good mind to complain to the Equal Opportunities Commission: they didn't get elves out after hours like that.

158

Then home to bed after midnight to find not even a cup of nectar left warm on the stove for her. Up again at the crack of dawn – well, almost – to do the Daily Inspection, as laid down in the Form 700, the Maintenance Schedule, for all those out-of-season flowers. How Tinkabell had the nerve to accept a Special Responsibility Allowance for looking after them when half the time she was off duty with unconvincing colds . . . or The Curse. It was no good. There were no silver linings anywhere.

She delved down into memory and dredged up another expression without which no gardener seemed able to work for long. 'Sod everything,' she said.

A couple of passing elves for fear crept into acorn cups and hid them there (traditionally the drill when angry fairies were encountered, swearing). Then this very morning she had discovered, too late, that her Cloak of Invisibility, admittedly only Mark 1 and getting threadbare these past three months, was suddenly quite impossible, so that she had had to borrow the cloak belonging to her younger sister (who would, surely, have given her permission had she been awake at that hour?). This was in good condition, true, but was a bit on the skimpy side: it offered her complete concealment only if she stood perfectly still and wrapped it around her. Movement was strictly out. So all morning she had had to creep from one flower to the next after first taking quite unprecedented precautions to make sure that she was unobserved. Fortunately at this time of the year – just approaching the winter solstice, though the humans had a different name for it – the Gardens were almost deserted, but still . . . Nerve-racking really. And now her bloody wand was on the blink. These transistorised models were supposed to go months without a battery change but new batteries had been fitted only a month ago – well, perhaps five weeks; that Servicing Department again. It had never been the same since they had gone over to computers. Perhaps her young brother was to blame: nobody had yet explained how the seven plaster g-nomës on the front lawn had come to life during the night and had been found the following morning stalking around in single file, singing some kind of ditty consisting largely of a repeated 'heigh-ho'. Something thought up by one Disni, she had heard.

Whichever way you looked at it, life was pretty putrid. She gloomed.

Along the path no more than a few feet away came mum, dad and daughter, the last aged perhaps six. Her underlip was set in a pout and her voice was raised in ceaseless, querulous complaint. 'Wanna go home,' she whined. 'Wanna watch Swopshop. (Swopshop: Wot dat?) It's cold. Wanna ice-lolly. Wanna go home...' And so on, ad nauseam.

After endless practice dad ignored her with ease. He strode on, several paces in front, clearly enjoying the bright sun, the fast-vanishing frost on the grass, the sparkle of water-drops hanging from the branches, the surging life of a new and untapped day. Mum, walking sideways so that she could address the brat, tried reasoning though she should, by now, have realised the futility of reason in such a situation. (After all, she herself had been a six-year old girl once and ought to have remembered what tactics would decidedly not work.) The fairy eyed the scene with distaste and thought that a swift right and left to those pretty little cheeks would quite certainly produce a much more satisfactory effect. Well, it would be satisfactory to *her*, anyway. Tears of anger were preferable to this mardy whingeing.

'Come along, dear,' mum tried brightly. 'Keep looking out for fairies. There are lots here, you know.'

'Fairies,' jeered the girl contemptuously. 'Don't believe in fairies. That's kids' stuff. Old-fashioned. Wanna go home and watch Saturday Swopshop. Wanna see Noel Edmonds.' (And who the hell was *he*, the fairy wondered.)

The child's voice trailed off in determined and sustained wails.

Right, thought the invisible watcher. Don't believe in fairies, hey? Well, you bleep, (there *are* limits, you know, even in straight reporting) you'll soon see. She pointed the wand and

160

with quick spurts of power undid the girl's left shoe-
lace, causing it to snake in and out of the eyeholes until a
respectable length was trailing. The right foot came down on
the lace; the left foot failed to lift but jerked forward and the
young harridan fell base over apex, not to put it more crudely
(although I could, gentle reader, I could easily), on to the gravel
path. There was an immediate shriek of genuine pain, a protest
against the basic unfairness of life.

Ha, thought the fairy: kids' stuff, hey? That's a nice bit of
gravel rash you have there, my girl. *Now* go home and watch
Swopshop with Whoeveritwas. That'll give you something to
cry for. With satisfied malevolence, and already feeling better
about life in general, she watched first aid being administered,
relished the cries and moans, and then ignored the family as
they retraced their steps towards the main gates.

From such heretical delights (the first Fairy Promise ran: 'A
fairy is a Friend to all young humans') the fairy was shocked
into sudden and full attention. A little knot of men had
approached her tree, ambling casually over the grass, and had
then stopped, made a loose circle and were now inspecting the
tree (*her* tree) from all angles. She checked that the cloak was,
in fact, on the job: all OK there. What then? Sit it out and wait
for them to go, obviously. But following a short appraisal there
were a few laconic remarks, some head-nodding, then two of
the men applied themselves to a huge saw and started to cut
down the tree. O Titania, the fairy though desperately: what
shall I do now? Move? Not possible: cloak too skimpy.
Persuade them it was time for a tea-break (a mysterious ritual in
which the gardeners sought regular solace, especially on winter
days): again impossible – wand still on the bloody blink. Break
cover and just leg it? Unethical: humans did not believe in
fairies and their innocence must be protected. While she was
thus threshing her stream of consciousness for a feasible plan of
action the tree lurched suddenly. The onlookers came forward
to support it and she used the opportunity to creep into the
crotch of a branch on the upward side; here she would be

161

invisible, being motionless. She could do nothing but hold on and await the incredible future.

The tree lurched wildly again and then assumed a horizontal position. The fairy found herself lying along the trunk, hanging on desperately to that bloody cloak and spitting out an occasional curse. There was some muffled to-you-from-me-ing and then with a rhythmic bouncing the tree started to move into the unknown. By now the fairy (her name, by the way, was Amanda) was thoroughly alarmed. No peace these days for a simple nature-spirit, she had long known, but whoever could have imagined a situation like this?

There was much else unprecedented to come. Who would have imagined a fairy riding in a tree in the back of an open lorry through the Christmas streets of Greater London? Or who would have imagined a genuine fairy in that home of the tawdry and the synthetic, a department store? As she was being carried in she tried to read the name over the door: it might give her a clue where she was now; but she only managed to make out 'Debe . . .' in very large letters on the facade and that meant absolutely nothing to her. Within an hour or so of leaving the gardens the tree had once again been reared on end, anchored on some kind of fastening, and was surrounded by hundreds of excited kids. By now Amanda's sense of vocation had taken quite a beating and the First Law was quite forgotten: she cursed them all quite comprehensively. Two shop-assistants mounted uncertain stepladders and busied themselves beschmucking the tree with tinsel, glass balls, streamers and presents-for-a-good-boy (wrapped in blue) or -for-a-good-girl (in pink). All this time the fairy clung motionless to the crotch, constantly checking the cloak and anxiously avoiding exposure to a startled world. A mixture of fright and disbelief and exasperation and incoherent anger and loneliness in this alien world. Forlorn, that's what she was, forlorn. The very word was like a bell. Now *that* was a nice thought but life was too fraught just now for Nice Thoughts. In any case she had never had any time for that Winifred Weak woman. Or was it? And in any case, *how was she going to get out of there?*

Yet the ne plus ultra of tragedy was yet to come. One of the shop girls, turning to descend the ladder for fresh supplies of plastic gaiety, clung briefly to a branch for support and the released branch, whipping back and forth before coming to rest, neatly hooked the Cloak of Invisibility and whipped it from her startled shoulders. Panic! But suddenly it was lunch time and without a backward glance at the tree the two girls cut imperatively through the crowd and vanished. At that precise moment, also, there was a commotion around the lifts and over all the turning heads Amanda could see the most spurious Saint Nicholas she could ever have imagined, surrounded by lashings of irrelevant but father's-eye-catching cheesecake, attractively unclad in vestigial garments of shimmering red trimmed with whiter-than-white, nylon-flavoured ermine. With great resource the fairy utilised this diversion: she shinned up a couple of feet of spiky trunk, playing hell with her gossamer-hose, and straddled the topmost spike of the tree. With her legs elegantly arranged and her left arm resting on the tip of the tree (nobody below could possibly have seen how tightly the fingers were gripping), and her right arm akimbo with the useless wand at Position Two, she was the loveliest fairy on a Christmas tree that anyone had ever seen or would ever see again.

And at that precise moment, just when a last quick wiggle ensured maximum comfort, she realised that one head, of all the many below, had been staring at her with unalloyed rapture. Daddy was clearly ogling Santa's entourage with undisguised carnal delight but Junior, aged perhaps four and of indeterminable sex, had never shifted an unflickering gaze from the tree. She winked brassily at him (her?) and hoped the little bastard would not kick up a scene. True, he would not be believed but if he persisted, someone might offer to take her down to convince him. She shuddered at the thought. Junior, however, was no fool. Even at such a tender age he knew what you couldn't explain to the adult world. He winked back, clumsily, his whole face creasing as he did so. It wasn't one of his more skilled attainments: one was merely surprised that he could do it at all. The operation was, perhaps, a prefiguring of campaigns yet to be fought. So when Dad tugged him to a position whence he, Junior, could the better appreciate the seasonal fun, Junior made no protest. A philosopher at an early age, he knew better than to spoil the occasion by clamouring either for adult recognition or for more of the same. Chase not too close the fading rapture, he thought, the unknown is life. (Or he would have thought it, given another year or so.)

Miss Matthews, back from lunch, cast a quick eye over her counter before turning to put the final touches to the tree. 'Eastern Promise', the counter was called: it did not, however, offer the Turkish Delight you might have expected. She checked: rose-candy, spikenard, mastic and terebinth and oil and spice, and . . . something still missing. What? Not jam: that belonged in Comestibles, in the basement. She glanced at the tree and stiffened in annoyance: that old bag from Lingerie had come back early from lunch and had placed a large and garish fairy at the top of the tree. Some people . . . Crawlers, that's what. Making eyes at the new new Floor Supervisor – Captain something-or-other; thought the sun shone out of his . . . Christmas spirit, indeed: anyone could see that the thing was in dreadful taste. Cheap and nasty, she thought.

A few minutes later the Old Bag from Lingerie – known to her friends, the management and her Income Tax Inspector as Mrs Jenkins – also arrived back from lunch. In her hand she carried a fairy for the top of the tree: a common-or-garden, oo-isn't-it-lovely type of fairy. Indeed, it might well have been quite lovely by ordinary standards but it was not to be compared with the fairy already there. Mrs Jenkins was furious, but absolutely *furious*. She knew at once what had happened, of course: that old cow in Eastern Promise had come back early from lunch and done it, had placed this inferior substitute where it had no right to be. Everyone knew that decorating the tree had always been the responsibility of Lingerie. Then when the Floor Supervisor came around she would draw attention to it – discreetly, of course – and wait for the plaudits. With that silly simper on her face. She glanced across: Miss Matthews caught her eye and each glared at the other in justified indignation. It was a glare of mutual hatred, naked, almost enough to sizzle the air through which it passed.

Into this explosive situation came, all unwittingly, the new Floor Supervisor; after all, he was only a man and so could not comprehend either these feelings or their origins.

Approaching Miss Matthews he offered, 'What a lovely tree. And the fairy looks absolutely enchanting.'

He was mildly surprised to elicit only a cold, 'Really?', a sniff and a receding back. Summing up the situation quickly, and wrongly, he went over to Mrs Jenkins, now languidly re-arranging her counter and repeated his remark.

'Some people might like it,' she observed haughtily, 'but to people of taste it's quite clearly overdone. Tawdry, I think.' Again he was left facing a hostile back.

'Bloody women,' he thought, for the thousandth time in his career. Nobody would ever understand them. Always at each others' throats. Until a man took sides, of course, and then they stood shoulder to shoulder and did their best to tear him to pieces. He shook his head sadly and wandered away.

So all through the busy, noisy afternoon the fairy clung to the top of the tree while the crowds swirled around and the hot air rose in waves and electronic noise (music? really?) battered at overstretched nerves. Overtired or frustrated children grizzled and whined (diplomacy continued by other means) and irritable parents snapped and threatened and jerked so wildly at small arms that it was a wonder that arm and body did not part company. The staff became progressively more exasperated, the shelves emptier and the floor more littered. Six o'clock: the winter evening settled down with smells of stale fried onions from the Quick Burger Bar and wet clothing (it had been raining outside) and the occasional premature stink bomb from

165

the Party Novelties counter ('All your friends will just *roar*').
The long day drew to a belated close.

Just about then the fairy checked the output milliammeter for
the hundredth time and thought that the wand might be having
a brief, if insecure, period of serviceability: by now she was
desperate enough to run any risk, so with the aid of its flickering
powers she conjured herself to a protruding ledge, conveniently
near to an open window. Within seconds she was outside again,
enjoying the cold but clean evening air. Her defection was
unnoticed: attention was now only for dust-sheets and last
minute ditherers, trying desperately to decide between the rival
attractions of table-mats, fancy tea-towels and gift-tokens.

An endless stream of buses passed along the High Street and
at the end of the alley where the fairy now found herself there
was a convenient stop; with a spurt of hope she noticed that one
of the routes went to Kew. Now if only . . .

It took her half an hour, via a heavy shopping-bag and with
the aid of another spurt of power from that bloody wand. The
bag was stowed safely and snugly under the stairs and when the
owner retrieved it a few stops further on the stowaway was
ensconced in the dark angle, far back under the stairs. All went
well until a later passenger proposed to push a couple of bulky
holdalls into the space and in order to make room moved
another bag already there. O fat white woman whom nobody
loves why must you hump around two bags of that size? The
conductor saved the day. Coming down briskly from the the top
deck ('Hurry along there please. Both sides on. Plenty of room
on top. Come on, then, Ma') he found preliminary manoevres
in progress without the necessary ritual placations. He pointed
to the notice with one grimy thumb and said, 'You can't get that
in there, missus. Have to wait for the next bus.'

'But there's plenty of room,' protested the passenger, and
quite rightly.

The argument, however, was not about the amount of
available space: it was about who was the boss on that bus and
the passenger had to lose. But she was no meek Southron: she

166

positively enjoyed a good Northern fight (strictly on grounds of principle, of course). Not for nothing had she been very largely brought up by her aunt, who had been a prominent and combative Member of Parliament for a northern constituency.

Her opening gambit was to refuse to move the first of her bags from its position, half on and half off the loading platform; the other severely obstructed the way for other passengers trying to board. Her opponent, not unmoved by the thought and sight of the growing tail of traffic behind the stationary bus, made some show of checking the available luggage space. He bent down and poked his head into the aperture, looking towards the angle of the stairs. With his torso thus bent at right-angles, he stiffened: in the dusty gloom was a blur of intense light and, as his eyes refocussed, there in the middle of the aureole was an unmistakeable fairy. For a moment his mind raced wildly; his mouth hung gently opened. Then he uncoiled himself and faced the passenger again.

'Sorry,' he said (a major concession in itself). 'Like I said, there isn't enough room.' (Could he take it home for the kids? Would it sting? Did you have to have a licence? What would you feed it on? Could they put it in with the budgy? Who was going to believe him? Was it really there? Was he losing his marbles?)

The fat woman stood implacable beside her bags and gripped the rail firmly. 'J'y suis,' she announced. 'J'y reste.'

Well, not really: what she actually said was, ' 'Ere I am and 'ere I stay.' Had she ever heard of MacMahon? She looked as if she meant it, too, and clearly she was going to take some shifting.

The conductor admitted defeat: he rang the emergency signal. The driver needed no prompting: for several minutes he had been fretting over the inaction – indeed, one or two impatient motorists had begun to hoot querulously. He emerged from his cab, stamped round to the back of the bus and filled the platform to overflowing.

'Wasser marrer?' he demanded.

'Passenger wants to put her bags under the stairs and it's full.'

'Righto, Ma. You heard what the conductor said. Have to wait for the next bus. There'll be one along in a minute. Can't keep all these people waiting. We're late already.'

'But there's loads of room under there,' she protested. 'You have a look.'

The driver looked mutely at the conductor. The passenger was, of course, wrong – even if there was nothing at all under the stairs. The conductor looked at him helplessly, put his lips close the driver's right ear and said, as softly as he could; 'You can't put anything under there, Alf. There's a fairy under there.'

For a moment longer the driver's face retained its usual stolid incomprehension, then his jaw sagged slightly. He frowned and turned his head to eye the conductor. The latter flushed slightly under his coating of London tan and refused to meet his mate's eyes. For some few seconds they stood thus motionless until the driver, too, stooped and looked under the stairs. He remained in that position rather longer than might have been expected for such a routine check, then he straightened up and spoke to the passenger with unusual and irresistible force. That lady, dazed, found herself standing on the pavement with her bags, and was left looking after the vanishing lights of the bus before she remembered that she had not had a chance to take a number for her inevitable complaint.

The bus now bowled on its way at the head of a sizeable column. Neither member of the crew had his mind on his job: for each duty was merely a Pavlovian reaction while the mind busied itself with other, incredible, things. At every stop the conductor stood both defensively and obstructively before the luggage stowage, and with his presence and his look deterred other passengers from any attempt to dispose of baggage in the place officially provided.

Eventually the bus reached Kew and, having discharged the last passengers, turned around ready for the return journey. In the general shemozzle the fairy wanded herself into yet another shopping basket and soon hopped out smartly into the nearest shrubbery. Her feet were killing her. What she wanted was a good cup of hot nectar. What her sister was going to say about the missing cloak was nobody's business. One thing: she would jolly well tell the storekeeper and the supervisor what she thought of the servicing department. Give her the old-fashioned wands any day. This new-fangled rubbish . . . Probably Japanese or something, if the truth were told. And that Tinkabell had jolly well better be fit for work tomorrow: if anyone needed a day off, it wasn't Tinkabell. Still, what a story to tell the others in the dorm.

And so, rehearsing her story and balancing life's burdens against its compensations, she leaves us.

When the last passenger had left and the lights had been turned off, the conductor made a great show of checking that nobody had left anything behind, just like it says in the rule-book, after all. Nothing on the top deck. Nothing on the lower deck. Nothing in the parcel stowage . . . Nothing? Then what? The driver came around, clearly pregnant with thought but baffled by British phlegm and convention and his own two size eleven feet, firmly planted in the commonsense world. He looked mutely at his mate.

'Everything OK,' said the conductor, refusing to meet the driver's eye. For a short moment, only, they paused before they went off to the tea-stall as usual.

The Gardens were still, ruffled only by a gentle evening breeze. Whatever life they held was hidden by darkness – and by disbelief.